The Morticians' Gambit

A Rock Paxton Novel

C.B. Wiland

authorHOUSE®

AuthorHouse™
1663 Liberty Drive, Suite 200
Bloomington, IN 47403
www.authorhouse.com
Phone: 1-800-839-8640

First published by AuthorHouse 11/18/2008

ISBN: 978-1-4389-1950-8 (sc)
ISBN: 978-1-4389-1954-6 (hc)

Library of Congress Control Number: 2008909212

Printed in the United States of America
Bloomington, Indiana

This book is printed on acid-free paper.

The events described herein are the products of the author's imagination as are the names and descriptions of any character living or dead. Such is purely coincidental.

Other Novels by the Author

The Pygmy

The Survivors' Affair

Ethan's Son

The Unattended Passion

Death on Hold

The Affair of the Mayan Princess*

Azrael: Angel of Death

* A sequel to the Survivors' Affair

Dedication

Dedicated to all who still enjoy a quiet evening at home with a work of fiction and to all who seek relief from the pervasive intrusion of the electronic world--the land of Jabberwocky, which leaves nothing to the imagination. Here's to the diminishing few who still find leisure- time pleasure in the written word--printed on acid free paper, of course.

Prologue

(Rock Paxton's ruminations from the final page of
Azrael: Angel of Death)

So it is. April has gone to London and left me with good and bad memories. As I poke around in those memories, I'm convinced that I've learned more about being a man from the bad than from the good. Perhaps it takes the bad to make a man.

I'm writing this at a small desk--Midge calls it secretary--in a room off our bedroom. My bride, the mighty one, says the room will house our babies. My little bride, it seems, has large ambitions. Babies! I'd lived alone for the last ten years. Now I have Midge and as yet an undetermined number of rug rats. I'm not complaining. If it's a boy, We'll call him Rock. A girl, April, even if she comes in May or June.

As I write, the soft light in the small room reaches Midge's lovely face. Tears come to my eyes as I ask myself how I could be so lucky. Her eyes open, she smiles, and asks seductively, "Are you coming to bed soon?"

Rock Paxton

Characters

The Mortician - (Mort) and Marian (The name given to Mort's female accomplice).

Lt. Luis Agosto - The head of homicide.

Adrianna Cromwell - Owns the Loving Shepherd Cemetery and Mortuary.

Peter Cromwell - Adrianna Cromwell's CPA husband.

Nan Delacorte - Rock's tall, tough, sassy, and well-built partner.

Mary O'Malley - The Mortician's first human victim.

Martin and Louisa Parnell - Owners/operators of Parnell's Funeral Home.

Dr. Sheri Samuelson Parnell - Victor Parnell's wife and an instructor at the Samuelson College of Mortuary Science.

Victor Parnell - Son of Martin and Louisa and manager of the Parnell family's crematory.

Brad (Rock) Paxton - Lead investigator in the Mortician murders.

Denise Paxton - Rock's stepmother. A welcome surprise.

Donna (Midge) Paxton - Rock's wife. The Mighty One.

Ron Paxton - Rock's contractor father.

William (Billy) Rockefeller - A panhandler with an expensive hobby. The second Mortician murder.

Dr. Dustan Samuelson - CEO of the Samuelson College of Mortuary Science.

Dustan Samuelson, Jr. - The doctor's son who procures cadavers for the college.

Nina Samuelson - Dustan Junior's wife.

Georgia Selby - Computer Science instructor. Wm. Rockefeller's landlady and heir.

Hernando Wright - Lt. Luis Agosto's nephew who goes undercover for his uncle.

Part One

When compassion overrides rational boundaries, it may enter the realm of whimpering sentimentality, and lead to the perversion of honest and realistic interaction between men and women of good will.

C. B. W - 08

1

"Wow. There are some real sickos out there," Midge said, sticking out her very pink tongue and making a yucky face.

Sitting in our newly acquired Lazy Boy recliner, I glanced up, caught the expression, said with minor enthusiasm, "Really," and returned my full attention to the TV. The Tampa Bay Rays were playing the Yankees in New York. It was the bottom of the ninth and the Rays were leading by a single run. The pin striper's two-hundred and-twenty-eight-million dollar man--Alex Rodriguez--was at bat with a two strike, two ball count and the bases loaded. A walk would tie the game. Any deep hit would end it with a Yankee win. A third strike would end it in favor of the good guys.

Percival, the Rays grizzled closer, was on the mound. He wound up and delivered a slow-breaking curve. I twisted in my chair, attempting to compel a swing from Alex. The ball broke low and outside. Ball three. A full count. I leaned forward, a thumb nail clenched between my front teeth, as Percival--from the stretch--released a fastball. "It's too good," I mumbled. The pitch broke down and in and crossed the inside corner of the plate at the knees. Strike three called. It was over. The money man had lost his battle with the grizzled veteran. He'd probably win the next time. But this one was ours, and I was exhausted.

I turned off the set after watching Percival being mobbed by his Ray team mates, and Alex stare angrily at the umpire before returning to the dugout. I looked at Midge and said, "Well, it's over. We won."

"Really," she said, avoiding my eyes by staring at the Tribune.   Then she said, "I don't understand what you see in that silly game."   She spit each word out as though it had a bad taste. I knew she was miffed. Teed off. During the first six months of our marriage, I'd never been the object of her anger. I was now. However, as I looked at her, I realized I had probably angered her before and hadn't noticed. I had this habit of drifting off to my private never-never land. Not hearing. Not seeing. Not communicating. Just me and my thoughts.

I left my recliner and settled beside her on the couch. "You're upset," I said.

"You really think so? Why on earth would I be upset?"

"Because I sort of ignored you."

"You sort of ignored me? My, you certainly have a way with words. Perhaps you should write poetry."

I slid one arm under her shoulders and the other under her thighs and lifted her to my lap. She resisted as I tried to turn her face to mine. Rigid. Cold.

"So sorry," I said as I tried a second time. She turned slowly and there were tears in her beautiful eyes. I kissed her eyes gently and repeated my apology. Then she grudgingly surrendered her lips. Three more kisses and we'd moved from the Arctic Circle to the Amazon Basin. Hot. Steamy. I was forgiven. Big time. In spades.

After several more kisses, I came up for air—reluctantly—and asked, "What did you say that I so rudely ignored?"

"Oh that," she said like it was of no importance now, "I said that there are some real sickos out there."

"Really. And what in the Tribune brought out that very astute observation?"

"Astute observation?"

"Teasing," I said.

"Well...a sick poodle belonging to an old couple in Plant City disappeared last week."

"That's sick?"

"Hush. Let me finish."

"Go," I said

"It reappeared on their front steps three days later."

"And they rejoiced by singing the Hallelujah Chorus?"

"Smart ass," she said.

"Finish," I said.

"It was dead...and had a pink ribbon around its neck."

"And?"

"It had been embalmed."

"Embalmed?"

"Yes."

"That's sick."

"Who would do something like that?" she asked.

"A mortician," I said, stating what seemed to be the only plausible answer. After which I added, "Or a sicko." That seemed to please her. She smiled and nodded. I had validated her original conclusion way back when. My slight had been completely forgiven.

* * *

It was Sunday afternoon. We always went out for dinner on Sunday evening. "What time is our dinner reservation?" I asked.

"Six thirty...same as always."

After glancing at my watch, I said, "We still have two hours. Should we?"

She smiled. I picked her up and headed for the bedroom and the still unmade bed, unmade because we always loafed around and did other amusing things on Sunday afternoons before dinner. After all, we were newlyweds—relatively speaking.

* * *

The alley was lighted only by a single bulb over a receiving dock at the far end of the black,dismal cavern. A mixed breed cur—mostly beagle—cowered in fear beside a garbage receptacle. It was one of the places where the dog regularly scrounged for sustenance. It was also one of the places where the Mortician sought out the dregs of the city's animal population--the emaciated, the flea and tick bitten, and the scabby. In a mission shared by his wife, the Mortician's alleged objective was to rescue such dying creatures from a slow death and give them peace. But there was more to it.

With his flashlight beam pinning the cowering animal against the wall, the black clad rescuer approached it, speaking softly. The dog crouched and waited, his scabby ears touching the pavement. When the Mortician was within a few feet of the animal, he laid a wiener on the pavement, backed off, and waited.

"I won't hurt you. The meat's yours. Come on, you filthy little bitch."

The animal inched forward, the odor of the wiener was a powerful, irresistible magnet. Suddenly, he scooted forward, grabbed the wiener, and returned to the corner formed by the wall and the garbage receptacle.

A second wiener was laid a few feet closer. He crawled forward, grabbed and devoured it on the spot. Fear conquered by starvation, he looked up, offered a feeble wag of gratitude, and waited. A third wiener was all his shrunken stomach would accept, He tried a fourth, choked and dropped it. But three had done the job. He tried to walk away, stopped, and toppled over. Tongue out. Eyes closed.

The dark man leaned over the unconscious stray. "Sleep my little friend. No more garbage cans, kicks, cold nights, disease, flea and tick infestations. Soon you'll be home. At peace." Tears from his eyes fell on the animal's heaving chest.

Wrapping a blanket around the dog, he carried it to the end of the alley where his idling Volvo was parked. He opened the trunk and placed the animal on a second blanket that lined the interior.

2

The Mortician left Tampa on Route 301 and headed northeast toward the farm he and his wife owned twenty miles from the city. The farm wasn't truly a farm. Flowers for their dinner table were the only things they raised. It was a retreat, a peaceful haven given to her by a loving father as a graduation gift ten years earlier. Their primary residence was a condo on Tampa's waterfront.

Upon reaching the farm, the Mortician followed the driveway past a small house and drove to the nearest of three outbuildings to its rear. He paused in front of the overhead door, pressed the remote button that opened it and turned on a row of overhead fluorescent light units. Once inside, he drove into the parking bay, set the brake and closed the door. He had parked beside a metal-sheathed door set in an interior concrete block wall. Taking a key from an inside jacket pocket, he opened the metal door and returned to the Audi for his frail captive.

"Here we are critter. No more fleas for you." He picked up the animal and placed him on a hospital gurney that stood against the wall next to the door. He wheeled the animal into the room, a brightly lit, sterile, and fully equipped mortuary.

The laboratory, designed and equipped by her—his spouse—to implement her passion for canines. It was a passion that involved rescuing sick and dying animals from the streets or from area animal shelters. And, after caring for them until they joined their ancestors, preparing them for the afterlife by embalming and burying them in a small cemetery to the rear of the property. Death with dignity for her favorite creatures.

Next to one wall of the mortuary was a two-by-seven-foot plywood box with a hinged top and an eight-square-inch glass viewing port at one end. This was his creation, a chamber designed to hurry the dying along. He opened the lid and laid the sedated dog on the padded bottom. Closing the lid, he checked the connections on a hose leading from the exhaust of a small gasoline engine to a second connection in the bottom of the plywood box. Then he started the engine.

Through the viewing glass, he watched the dog's labored breathing as the lethal carbon monoxide fumes poured into the chamber. Five minutes passed. Another two minutes and the breathing stopped. It was over. No more suffering. No more hunger. Satisfied with his evening's work, the Mortician turned off the engine and left the mortuary. He'd finish later.

As he walked toward the brick bungalow that fronted the property, an outside light came on. She was waiting for him as always. He was so fortunate to have found someone who, among other things, adored him. She was brilliant, beautiful, and malleable, which—from his perspective—was the best of her traits.

She'd exhibited her beautiful body in PETA protests on several occasions, and had caught his eye at one such demonstration on Franklin Street near City Hall. Of course, that stopped after their marriage. Although he didn't question her right to participate in such protests, the thought of her appearing nude in public was more than he could bear, no matter the cause. Her body was his to prize, admire, and—putting it bluntly—to use at will.

After that first sighting, he'd known that he had to have her. He had followed her for several days and finally cornered her at a Humane Society gathering. They'd talked and talked and—after the meeting—they'd agreed that they were so much in tune that they shouldn't delay going to bed together. So they did. That very night.

As it worked out, he became her willing partner in collecting, euthanizing, embalming, and burying the hapless animals that roamed the city and its suburbs. She always found time to plant and care for the flowers in the small cemetery she'd created.

It had been on the night he brought the emaciated poodle home several days earlier that they made the decision to take their crusade public. They decided that public officials needed to be shocked into action in behalf of unwanted animals. Of course he had other motives for going public that he failed to mention at the time. It was his little secret.

* * *

Another Sunday arrived, the Sunday after our little brouhaha over the embalmed poodle. I was caught up in the sports section reviewing what I already knew about Saturday's activity. I'd caught ESPN at midnight.

I heard Midge sneak from the bathroom and pretended not to hear her creeping down the hallway toward the family room where I was ensconced.

Suddenly, she was on my back like a wildcat in heat—which she was under certain conditions. Wrapping her arms around me from behind, she bit my ear and said, "Finally it's happened. I tested positive."

Always the joker, I said, "What did you test positive for, sweetheart? Hepatitis B?"

"Don't tease, Rock. I'm pregnant. I am pregnant."

After a second choke hold and another bite on my ear, she slid around and dropped her massive one-hundred-and-five pound body onto my lap.

"How on earth did that happen?" I asked.

"You took advantage of me," she said and bit my lip.

"I did?" I said, attempting to sound indignant. "I thought it was the other way around. Please explain your accusation."

"You want a demonstration?"

"I've already had several robust demonstrations during the past six months."

"Several? How about one-hundred-and-eighty, you savage."

"You've been counting," I said and pinched her bottom. "Have you been putting notches on the headboard? Of course you have. And…second question… do you take notes?"

"Answer to your second question…only after a spectacular performance"

I glanced at my watch. "Are we going to the second service this morning?"

"Why?"

"It would give us an extra hour."

"To do what?"

"Whatever," I said as I picked her up and headed for the inner sanctum.

3

The mayor almost stepped on the bundle that lay next to her morning Tampa Tribune. Startled, she stepped back into the house and called her husband. There was an element of fright in her voice. Getting no immediate response, she called again. Louder. A third call brought her sleepy-eyed spouse to her side. He was sipping a cup of Don Francisco Columbian and wearing a terry-cloth robe. A late night poker game made the coffee a necessity for survival. The robe, also a necessity since he slept in the buff.

"What?" he said.

"That," she said, pointing to the bundle lying on the porch.

"What in the hell…"

"Yes. What in the hell. My sentiments exactly."

"Here," he said, reluctantly handing her his cup.

"It could be dangerous...a bomb."

"Doubt it. Don't think the Kazinskys of this world wrap their bombs in baby blankets. Probably a neighbor kid's doll. Step back... though...while I take a peek."

"Be careful..."

"Most certainly, my love." He lifted the corner of the blanket and frowned at what he saw.

"What is it?"

He pulled the blanket completely open, exposing the Mortician's latest handiwork. "See for yourself."

She leaned over his shoulder. "A dog. It's a dog."

"Damned sure is...an emaciated, mangy bastard." The mixed breed, mostly beagle, looked very comfortable in death. He was on his belly, head resting on his paws. His ears touched the brick stoop. He was very clean and the aroma of a scented shampoo rose from his sparse fur. An envelope was pinned to a blue ribbon around his neck.

"He is dead, isn't he? Not just drugged? There's something pinned to...."

"Yes, he's very dead and I see the envelope." He removed the envelope from the ribbon, opened it, and read the note inside. After reading it, he handed the note to her with a smile and a comment. "Looks as though some animal lover doesn't think you're doing your job."

"I'll be damned," she muttered several times as she read the Mortician's message:

Mayor:

I found this poor animal scrounging for food in one of our filthy downtown alleys. I've given him peace. It's all I could do for him. People who turn animals loose to roam the streets and starve should be incarcerated. But you might have to put one of your constituents in jail. Couldn't do that, could we? And a countywide neutering/spading program would unbalance the city and county's budgets I suppose. Just leave it up to animal control and starvation. Right. Hundred's of starving people and animals around, but as long as your gut's full, who cares. I don't know how such callous people can be elected in a civilized society. But then, who says we're civilized? Shame, shame on you and the commissioners. Correct the problem or unpleasant things may happen. The Mortician

"Obviously one sick s.o.b.," he said from where he still knelt beside the animal. "Something you should know."

"Yes?"

"Damned misfit has embalmed this pathetic beast, ergo, the Mortician."

"Relatively harmless, I suppose, as long as he sticks with animals," she said.

"As the Bard would say 'and there's the rub' or something like that. The guy does refer to starving people in his little billet doux."

"Billet Doux? Hardly."

"About this possible elevation to a higher species, maybe you should alert…that guy…the head of Major Crimes. Damned if I can remember his name."

"Beryl Tankersly," she said. "Uh…dear."

"Yes?"

"Your memory shortfall is beginning to bother me."

"I can't remember one damned name, and you think I'm senile."

"We've had Beryl to dinner three times."

"So? I do have a shortfall. A block. May I please have my coffee before I forget what it's called."

* * *

Three weeks after delivering the dead animal to the Mayor's doorstep, the Mortician sat in the rear of the Parnell Funeral Home's small chapel. One of a sparse gathering of mourners, he was there to observe the rites for one Terrence T. O'Malley. It was after reading O'Malley's brief obituary that he'd decided to attend the service:

Mr. Terrence T. O'Malley, 87, a native of Watertown New York, died Monday at his residence after a long illness. Mr. O'Malley's only survivor is his widow, Mary. The service will be held Thursday, March 27 at 3 p.m. in the small chapel at Parnell's funeral home. In lieu of flowers, a fund to assist Ms. O'Malley with expenses has been established by friends and neighbors. Call 813-9222 for information.

His plans for the future began to take shape when he read the simple obituary. He smiled now as he watched an attendant assist the tiny, frail wife of Terrence O'Malley to the open coffin. There, she leaned over and placed an arthritic hand on her husband's head and gently stroked his silver hair. Then, she collapsed. On her knees, her hands gripping the edge of the casket, her shoulders shook with sobs until the attendant helped her to her feet and escorted her back to her place in the front pew.

It was all he needed. He'd seen enough. Quietly, he rose from his seat and left the funeral home. He trembled with excitement when he thought about parlaying his ostensible compassion for animals to the Mary O'Malley's of the city and moving the overriding plan along.

4

The Mortician looked at his wife as he chewed a piece of medium rare prime rib a jus. "It was horrible, dear. A frail, elderly woman who could barely walk…weeping at her husband's casket …stroking his hair. Destitute. No children. A bleak future to say the least. I checked her hovel of a residence. A mobile home in a run down trailer park." He shook his head, sighed and managed a sad smile. "By the way dear, the prime rib is perfect…as always."

After thanking him for the compliment, her face became solemn as she joined him in his anguish over the bleak future of Mary O'Malley, widow of the late Terrence O'Malley. She wanted to assure him that she shared his deep empathy for all of God's desolate and abandoned creatures, although—in all honesty—her main concern was canines. Always had been since she'd gotten her first terrier pup at age four. She'd called him "Dipsy" because of his silly antics.

They finished their meal. She went to the kitchen and returned with a carafe of freshly-brewed coffee. After pouring, she rejoined him at the table. He took a sip of the rich Colombian brew and cleared his throat.

"Yes, dear. You've something on your mind?" She asked.

"I'm amazed. You read me like my thoughts were in lights on a theater marquee. Am I that...predictable?"

"What is it, dear?"

"Well...I've been thinking. Why should we limit our mission of mercy to stray dogs? Are only canines being mistreated...only canines worthy of release from the horrors of a marginal existence?"

"I don't believe I like where you're going. Not at all."

"Oh. Perhaps you believe that dogs are more worthy of compassion than humans."

"Dogs can't speak for themselves. Most humans could care less about stray animals."

"Most could care less about stray humans."

"I don't believe that...there are many, many agencies and programs to assist destitute and ill humans."

He stared at her and put on his most forlorn face. The one that brought out her mothering instincts "Oh, well. I guess we aren't as together on certain things as I thought we were. Just forget I said anything. I'll just take your reluctance as a refusal and move on." He tipped his head back and focused his eyes on the chandelier suspended over the table. Tears filled his eyes.

"I...I didn't say no," she said.

"And you didn't say yes," he said and continued to stare at the chandelier.

"We'd...we'd have to be...very careful."

"Of course," he said. Now he looked at her. There were tears now in her exquisite eyes. Tears over her failure to please him. She loved him so—and he knew it.

"They'd call us murderers. Dr. Death...Kavorkian... was jailed for helping people die...for helping them do what they asked him to do."

"We'd be helping those who don't have the courage to ask." His eyes were shining with new zeal. An expanded mission was in the offing. The plan had moved another giant step forward. He'd have to share the news.

"I suppose...I suppose you could justify it that way."

Sensing his complete victory, he said, "Are you willing to work with me on this, darling?"

"It's a serious departure from euthanizing unwanted animals, but if you promise to be very, very careful."

"We shall be very, very careful, knowing that the insensitive, stiff-necked bastards who dictate social morality will call us murderers. But where are they...these moralists...when the best option an uncaring society offers these unwanted and abandoned creatures is slow, painful death."

"I trust your judgment ,dear, but...but I am afraid. Very afraid."

The Mortician shook his head. "Afraid? Afraid of serving the helpless? Afraid of being called a murderess? My sweet, we must only worry about those who need help. We must not worry about society's stupid, uncaring perspective."

"We...we could give it a try, I suppose," she said.

He savored a moment of silent pleasure over her concession, before saying what he had in mind all along. "Should we offer a peaceful departure to Mary O'Malley as a start?"

"From what you've said about her, it would appear to be…a good thing…a merciful thing to do," she said. "Why don't we invite her to dinner next week at our place in town and find out more about her...before we make a final decision."

"Splendid. I think it best that you approach her…for reasons of trust. You being a woman…a beautiful one. I'll give you her address. Why don't you fix prime rib again? It would provide a splendid send off if we decide it's the right thing to do." He already knew what the right thing to do was, and he knew that he would prevail as always.

5

It was just after dark. She knocked on Mary O'Malley's door several times before hearing the soft pad of slippered feet approaching. A light with a broken glass cover came on above the door. Then the door cracked open.

"Yes. Who is it?"

"Ms. O'Malley. My name is Marian Knight. I'm a counselor with the Department of Human Services. Here's my card." She slipped the card through the crack in the door. It was something she dashed off on her computer upon deciding what her name would be. After a moment of silence, Mary responded.

"What is it, Miz Knight?"

"Could I come in, Mary? I'd like to discuss your situation with you. See if our agency can be of assistance.

I understand some of the neighbors have offered help. Perhaps we can do something more substantial."

That did it. Mary O'Malley opened the door and stepped aside, allowing the pleasant Miz Knight—a.k.a. Ms. Mortician—to enter. The world is full of good people, Mary thought, as she led her guest to an area at the far end of the small mobile home. A frayed and faded couch and a chair that would have looked better on the park's dump suggested that it was the trailer's living room. At Mary's invitation, Ms. Knight seated herself on the lumpy couch. Mary made her way to a caned chair over which a blanket was draped.

Each waited for the other to speak . Mary did the honors. "I'd offer you coffee, Miz Knight, but I'm a little short. Social Security check's late 'cause they're making a change, you know. I get Terry's check from now on…they told me."

"Please call me Marian. And I certainly don't need any coffee this late in the day. Keeps me awake. I'm not much of a coffee drinker anyway."

"Actually, I'm not really short, I'm out. My friend Nancy Brody's taking me to Publix when the check gets here."

"You shouldn't have to wait, Mary." Marian reached into her purse and retrieved an envelope. "Here's something to tide you over until your check comes."

Mary's eyes went from Marian's to the envelope and back. She offered a slight shake of her head, licked her lips, and said, "I really shouldn't take your money."

"Oh, Mary, this isn't my money. It's from a petty cash fund our office maintains to help folks in the short run. You'll have to give me a receipt before I leave."

"Well, in that case, I guess I can take it."

"Good. Now this neighbor…Nancy…does she live close?"

"First trailer on the other side of the trees as you come in the park. The place next door is empty. Owner died two months ago."

"How terrible to lose a neighbor. So close."

"Terry and him was good friends. Hit Terry hard."

"Look, Mary, I'm going to make a suggestion."

"Yes?"

"My husband enjoys meeting my clients. He's writing a book about how people handle tragedy. He'd love to talk to you about your situation. Would you please come to our place for dinner? Please. You're such a

31

sweet lady, and he's a very nice person. I adore him. You will, too. I just know you will."

* * *

I walked into the department's reception area and received my usual greeting from Sheila, the buxom, affable receptionist. Very white caps gleaming behind glossy red lips, she said, "Hi lover. You have a good weekend?"

"One of the best" I said and told her the good news about the pregnancy. A proud papa-to-be parading my remarkable feat. The world must know.

"I always suspected you'd be good at making babies."

"Good at making babies? It took six months. Hardly a record."

"That long? Maybe you needed more practice. You should have asked."

"For advice?"

"Do I look like Ann Landers...or her successor? I'm talking basic training. Hands on instruction. Rough and tumble stuff."

"That ever happens, could I bring Midge as a referee?"

"Spoil sport. Here." She faked a frown and handed me several case files I'd requested the previous Saturday. A Post-It note from department head Luis Agosto was stuck on the top folder. It was brief. "Rock. See me. A.M. L. A."

I dropped the files off as I passed my desk on the way to Lieutenant Luis Agosto's office. I knocked on the door, waited for an invitation, and entered when I received a brusque, "It's open. Don' t break the damn glass. Repair's not in the budget."

Agosto didn't look up from the report he was perusing. He managed to offer the canine command "Sit" while keeping his eyes on the report. Luis disliked paperwork—especially the CYA stuff dreamed up by politicians, prosecutors, and department brass. As soon as he cleared his desk, his demeanor would change. I'd seen it happen quite often during the three months since he'd taken over from Captain Dewayne Jackson who had retired.

I waited patiently for fifteen minutes. Several grunted expletives and a groan or two were the only communications from the wiry, bronze-skinned Lieutenant.

"I could come back, Lieutenant," I finally said.

"What?" He I looked at the clock over the door and grinned. "Sorry, Rock. Just finishing my monthly open case progress report. I get so damned caught up and excited doing the requisite reports I almost pee my pants."

"Thought you'd say you approach an orgasm."

"That too," he said and reached across the desk and shook my hand, his way of apologizing. It was almost impossible to dislike the dapper senior officer. At fifty-two, he could pass for forty-two. He smiled easily, but could be as tough as wang leather whip when he had to be. A full head of silver hair and a neatly-trimmed white mustache belonged on his lean, brown face.

When we'd been partners, I'd tried to emulate Luis by growing a mustache. It had turned out badly. I acquired a range of shades that would have been more appropriate on a calico cat...from very black to very brown with a gray spot dead center. I'd shaved it off the day some joker left a can of black shoe polish on my desk.

After an exchange of nothing much, I said, "Got your note, Lieutenant. What's up?"

"This." He pulled a folder from his bottom file tray and slid it across the desk. "You read about those embalmed dogs been left around town...one on the Mayor's stoop?"

"Midge told me about a poodle. Had a note that accused the owners of abusing it. Didn't hear about the one delivered to the Mayor."

"So, you were aware that the dogs...or dog...had been embalmed?"

"I heard....done by a some screwball who called himself the Mortician."

"Well, it seems that Mister Mortician has moved up from canines to homo sapiens. Here."

He handed me the report and kept talking while I tried to read the first responders' cryptic account. Finally, I gave up, leaned back and listened to Luis' rapid-fire summary.

"Neighbor lady and friend had arranged to take the victim shopping. Went to her place to gab and make arrangements for their shopping trip. She found this Mary O'Malley lying on her bed with a small bouquet of wild flowers in her hands."

"Embalmed?"

"You bet. With a note pinned to her dress."

"Saying what?"

Luis retrieved the file that lay on the desk in front of me and read from a copy of the note that was found on the cadaver. Forensics had the original:

Mayor and County Commissioners:
Here is another victim of your unfeeling disregard for the most helpless among us. Ms. Mary O'Malley, alone and living in squalor. Her husband dead. No children. Living on a pittance provided by a parsimonious government that has funds for an illegal war, for killing machines, and for politicians' pork but can't scrape up enough to care for our impoverished, our lonely and our disenfranchised. Mary's at peace now. But are you? How can you be? Shame. Shame. More later.   The Mortician

"One sick s.o.b, I'd say."
"One sick, dangerous s.o.b.," Luis amended.
"Could have been an assisted suicide," I said.
"Slight possibility, according to Bosch," he said, referring to the County M. E. "Even so, it would still be murder in Florida. Whatever, I want you and Delacorte to give it some thought. When you're ready, we'll meet and discuss an investigative strategy. Discuss personnel requirements, etceteras. Along those lines,

we don't have a homicide detective who isn't assigned elsewhere at the moment." I got the message. It's your baby, and there's no help in the offing.

Delacorte was a reference to my partner Nan Delacorte. Nan had caught major heat when a guy under her watch was hit by a perp calling himself The Angel of Death. She'd survived with minimal damage to her career.

"When should we report back?" I asked.

The Lieutenant glanced at his watch. It was 8:45 a.m. "How about after lunch? Say one o'clock."

"Damn generous. That should be plenty of time. Should we bring the Mortician in cuffs with us?"

"Think you can?" Luis smiled.

"Count on it," I said.

6

Delacorte and I got together a half hour after I left the Lieutenant's office. I had read the brief file and jotted down some observations. I was ready for my tall, lean partner who—among other very positive attributes— was intellectually sharp. After I summarized the contents of the dossier, she began asking questions.

"Dr. Bosch hasn't found the cause?" It was a reiteration of a fact from my summary.

"Not, yet. No obvious physical trauma...fractures, concussions, bruises, stab wounds."

"Toxic substances?"

"Embalming does a fairly complete job of eliminating evidence of toxic substances in body fluids..."

"Tissue analysis show anything?" she hurried on.

"Bosch is having tissue samples tested. Says suffocation's a possibility. Carbon monoxide poisoning very possible. Other toxins have been ruled out."

"Where's the body?"

"Bosch still has it. Says some tissue samples have been outsourced for advanced microscopy. Also, says they're typing the embalming materials for possible source identification."

"What does Bosch think of the embalming job?"

"Think?"

"Yes. Technique. Does it look like the work of a pro? Or a hatchet job by a nitwit who gets his kicks mutilating cadavers? Maybe he's an upscale taxidermist."

I didn't bother to comment about the differences between embalming and taxidermy since I didn't actually know much about either. She probably did. I let it stand to avoid embarrassment over my lack of erudition.

"Good thought, Nan. We should probably get an opinion from a professional mortician," I said.

"Where's the body going after Bosch is through?"

"I don't know," I said

"Let's find out," she said.

"I'll call," I said firmly. After all, it was my telephone.

* * *

We learned that the body was being released to the Parnell Funeral home, the firm that handled the funeral of Mary O'Malley's husband two week's earlier. We contacted Martin Parnell, the co-owner, and he assured us that he and his wife Louisa would examine the body and evaluate the professional competence of the—uh—mortician as soon as they received the body. Martin Parnell also advised us that Mary's neighbor had agreed to pay for the funeral. The neighbor's name was Nancy Brody, a widow. A merry one as we discovered later that day.

* * *

Nancy Brody answered the door as my knuckles were poised for a third knock. A lively, bright-eyed, trim sixty-or-so lady with impeccable coiffure and nails, she spoke with very precise diction. I pegged her as a retired professional of some sort. I learned later that I erred. She and her husband had owned an eighteen wheeler. She'd shared the driving on long hauls.

"You're police? Please come in."

"Thanks, Ms. Brody. We're here to..."

She cut Nan off. "Talk to me about Mary O'Malley... my dear friend."

As lead investigator, I stepped in. "That's it, ma'am. Can you spare some time for us? We could come back later, but we're most anxious to move our investigation along."

"The only thing I've got working is a fishing trip tonight with my boy friend, Jimmy," she said.

I scrutinized her carefully as she led us into the living room of the large doublewide. A boy friend? Of course. She was trim, shapely, and lively. Midge would probably look and act like Nancy Brody when she was sixty-or-so. It was a pleasant thought.

Nan and I shared a tapestry covered love seat. It felt and smelled new. Ms. Brody sat in a matching wingback chair, which was part of a grouping of furniture at one end of the room. All of the furnishings appeared to be new and expensive. It seems Nancy and her husband had done well in the trucking business.

"We'll keep it short, Ms. Brody." I said

"Nancy," she said.

"Yes. We'll keep it short, Nancy."

"Take your time, Detective." She batted her eyes and crossed her legs. I think I blushed but continued without an ogle.

"We understand that you discovered the body."

"Yes. I found the dear soul on Thursday morning. I was supposed to take her shopping the next morning. I knew she'd gone out for dinner on Tuesday evening..."

"Gone out for dinner?" Nan interrupted.

"Yes. With a woman from a social services agency. She stopped by...let's see...I found the body on Thursday...as I said. It was Monday. I didn't talk to her Monday. I saw her Tuesday morning, and she said this lady was picking her up at seven-thirty that evening."

"Did you see her being picked up?" I asked.

"No...well...I was at Jimmy's place Tuesday evening...for dinner and such." She blushed. The "and such" and the blush said it all. She continued, "Oh, she did give me the lady's card in case I wanted to call her."

"Do you still have the card?" I asked.

"Yes. I'll get it." She rose and went to a breakfront that graced a short wall on the far end of the room. She returned with the card and handed it to me.

I read the card aloud for Nan's sake. "Marian Knight, Grief Counselor, Department of Human Services." After reading the card, I slipped it into an inside jacket pocket and continued my interrogation.

"Ms...Nancy...according to the note that was with the body, Mary was destitute and very depressed. Was she considering suicide?"

Nancy laughed. Destitute? Depressed? She was happier than I'd seen her for over three years. Terry was a terrible burden. She didn't complain, but I could see it wearing her down. Changing his diapers. Bathing him. Feeding him. For three years since his stroke she did everything to keep him alive. His death was a blessing for her....and for him. Was a blessing for her financially, too. There was a five-hundred-thousand dollar insurance policy she was ready to cash in."

I looked at Nan. "Seems as though the Mortician wasn't well informed as to Mary's financial status."

"Also appears that the Mortician is either a woman or is working with one," Nan said.

"Could be a cross dresser," I said.

"Opens up a lot of avenues for investigation."

Nancy wasn't done talking. "Did you folks see the envelope that was pinned to her dress?" she asked.

"We only saw a copy of the note. Why?" Nan asked.

"It was addressed to the Mayor and County Commissioners. I didn't open it...you know because of latent prints."

"Very professional, Nancy, " I said. "Would you be interested in a job in homicide? I'd be very willing to recommend you."

"Would I be working with you?" She winked and giggled. She was indeed a Merry Widow. Lucky Jimmy.

7

"I believe I've found another unfortunate creature who could use our...uh...services," he said, slipping an arm over his wife's soft, elegant shoulders. They sat on a patio glider. He was turned on by the warmth of her body, her perfume, and the soft rise and fall of her breasts. The movement of the glider enhanced his mood. Back and forth. In and out. Back and forth. She was exquisite. In and out. Back and forth. In and out.

Her delayed response was brief. "Really," she said.

He ignored her lack of enthusiasm. "Yes. A ragged vagrant who stands at the Ybor City I-4 exit. Poor beggar has a sign saying that he'll work for food."

"An elderly man?"

"Hard to tell. Bearded. Wrinkled from sun exposure. Very thin."

"That's a very busy intersection. It could be extremely difficult to pick him up without being noticed. Perhaps…you should forget it."

"Yes…It could be difficult. There has to be a way, though." Back and forth. In and out. Back and forth.

"I suppose. You said you…we'd be careful."

"Are you having second thoughts about our mission of mercy?"

"It seems right. But I worry about being caught… and being misunderstood. I'm just not sure it's the right thing for us to do."

"I won't make a move until I'm certain."

"I know." She thought of Mary O'Malley on the mortuary table and shivered. The night air was damp. The lights of St. Petersburg's waterfront danced across Tampa Bay to where they sat on the second story deck of their condo. She moved closer to him for warmth, for reassurance.

"Let's go in, dear. It's chilly," she said.

"Yes…of course." They'd called him a geek in school. Tall. Awkward. Intelligent. Geek? If they could see her—see him now. He smiled and helped her to her feet. Back and forth. In and out. The sliding glass doors closed behind them as they escaped the clammy, night air and entered their bedroom.

* * *

After Martin and Louisa Parnell assured us that the Mortician or Morticians who'd embalmed Mary O'Malley were very professional, we prepared a list of licensed morticians in the county. The woman who had approached Mary O'Malley had mentioned her husband, so—until we learned differently—we assumed that a man and woman were involved in Mary O'Malley's permanent retirement. And, as suspected, we learned there was no one on the HRS staff named Marian Knight.

We decided to humanize these inhuman kooks by naming them Mort and Marian, rather than Mr. And Ms. Mortician.

After three weeks of looking into alibis and doing background checks, we reduced our list of potentials to those who—via written questionnaire--refused to submit to polygraph exams or whose responses seemed evasive:

Martin and Louisa Parnell – The co-owners of Parnell's Funeral Home. Their responses meshed like the gears on a Mercedes.

Victor Parnell, - Manager of the Parnell family's crematorium. He listed his wife as Sheri Samuelson, Dr. Dustan Samuelson's daughter,

Dr. Dustan Samuelson – Owner and President of Samuelson's College of Mortuary Science.

Dustan Samuelson, Jr.– Manager of the college's cadaver procurement, preservation, and disposition program.

Nina Samuelson – David's wife and assistant.

Dr. Sheri Samuelson Parnell - Daughter of Dustan senior, and wife of Victor Parnell. Anatomy instructor at the college.

Adrianna Cromwell – Owner/operator of the Loving Shepherd Cemetery and Mortuary, which she had inherited from her father.

Peter Cromwell – A CPA who assists in his wife's business part time. Not a licensed mortician, but wife has taught him what he needs to know to be helpful.

* * *

I left my desk early the day Nan and I finished sorting through our suspect list, arriving home around seven-thirty p.m. My usually upbeat friend, sweetheart, and very pregnant playmate greeted me with a gentle hug and a sad smile. Then she turned her back, and I put my arms around her and pulled her close.

"What's up, sweetheart?" I asked, kissing her neck.

"Your father wants to see you."

"That a reason to be so sad, miss sourpuss?"

"Oh, dear God," she sobbed. "He'll tell you."

* * *

For reasons that will become apparent later, it seems important that I tell you about my father, Ron Paxton. A wise man, a man who is gentle and considerate. I've never doubted his love for me and mother. He's been a successful commercial builder for over thirty years, an honest, hard worker who has met deadlines even if forced to fill in by carrying hod or laying block. He learned the business from his father and refined his knowledge and skills by taking community college courses and attending builders' conferences and local and state seminars on material standards, building codes, and etceteras.

Six foot and two hundred pounds, at fifty two, he's easily as physically strong as the younger men he employs. He has an unlined, square face, a full head of salt-and pepper hair, bushy eyebrows, and a nose that verifies time spent in Golden Gloves competition as a young man.

As must seem obvious, I love him. I love him as I've always known him—a strong, honest man, who laughs often and easily. A man who controls his temper in the most difficult circumstances and makes decisions that are well considered and just. He reads the bible daily and says that Solomon is his favorite of all Old Testament heroes. That's it. I should note I've written this in the present tense, so the reader will grasp the enormity of the change that came over this man I love so much.

* * *

Leaving Midge, I walked into Mom's kitchen, in itself a testimony to Dad's love of fine hardwoods and his skill as a cabinet maker. He was seated at the table, his eyes closed and his hands folded as if in prayer.

"What is it, Dad?" I asked. He didn't respond. I stood behind him and placed my hands on those hard shoulders and repeated my inquiry. "What's going on?"

He answered without opening his eyes or unclasping his hands. "It's Mother, Rock. It's Mom."

"What about Mom?" Something bad was coming. I felt hands gripping my throat. Pressure on my chest.

"Cancer," he said, "she has pancreatic cancer."

I knew very little about cancer, which became evident when I said, "Is it bad? They have new things... treatments...drugs that cure all sorts of cancers."

He turned in his chair, rose, and reached for my hands. Now his eyes were open. Vacant. Red. "Not... not this cancer, son. Doc's say it's...terminal." He sobbed and embraced me. I patted his back, I couldn't repress tears.

"How...how long do they say?"

"Two. Maybe three months." He was holding on to me now as though I had a better answer. I didn't.

"How is she taking it?" I asked.

"How has...has she always taken bad news?" He sobbed before adding, "Do you believe she smiled... kissed my hand, and said...let's make it our secret,

Ron dear. Let's not tell Rock and Midge. They have a child on the way. Let's not spoil it for them."

"God, that's my mother. Where is she?" I asked.

"On the library patio. Reading Grisham's latest novel."

8

He sat in a restaurant parking lot on the periphery of Ybor City and watched the scrawny little man with a multi-hued beard. The sign the man held said, "I'll work for food." He had been watching him off and on for two weeks. The traffic flow was down. Now, he was prepared to act. Climbing from a Ford Focus he'd rented in Orlando, he walked the block to where the ostensibly homeless wretch stood. The stalker stood facing the whiskered man with his back to the traffic.

"Hi, pard, how you doing?"

The man squinted at the casually dressed stranger. Doing whoever I can whenever I can. Who's asking? You a city guy…going to chase me off my spot?"

The stranger laughed. "Hell no. I noticed your sign and…well… I'd like to make you a proposition."

"Yeah? You some kind of pervert?"

The man laughed again. "Not that kind of proposition, friend. It's this way. My wife and I have a little farm north of here. We both work in town, and we need someone to house sit for two weeks until our regular... a neighbor kid...returns from a trip to Italy."

"I'm not much of a house sitter, man. I like to keep moving."

"You like to keep moving so much, why've you been on this corner for over a month?"

The vagrant's grin displayed some remarkably good teeth. "You've seen me here, huh?"

"Yeah, I've seen you." They both laughed. Then the stranger asked, "How much do you make doing what you're doing? How much a day?"

"A day? Between sixty and seventy bucks most days. I have regulars who give me five or ten bucks a day."

The stranger smiled and pulled out his wallet. "How does eighty a day and twenty a day for food and whatever else sounds good to you? Two weeks in advance and another twenty a day when our regular returns, and I bring you back to your corner."

"You offering me a hundred a day plus to watch a house?"

"Yup. Watch the house and feed two cats. We'll provide the cat food."

"How do you know you can trust me?"

"For starters, you'll be living in a small apartment in one of our outbuildings. Second, the house has a very good security system. You won't have the code, but the police and fire departments will. Last, you may want to do it again someday for the easy money."

The vagrant glanced at the stranger's fat wallet and licked his lips. "I'll think about it. Tell you tomorrow."

"Can't wait," the man said while returning his wallet to an inside jacket pocket. "I'll get someone at Manpower." He turned to walk away.

"Hey, man. I didn't say no."

"You haven't said yes."

"Okay, Okay. I'll do it. What's your name, man?"

"Franklin Graham. What's yours?"

"Billy," the street corner beggar said with a chuckle.

* * *

After a lovely meal of ribs, baked beans, and sweet corn—skillfully prepared by Marian—Billy, their itinerant guest, burped and passed out with a contented grin on his shaggy face. Mort smiled and said, "Very well done, dear."

"May I say something?"

"Of course."

"Must we go through with this...put him to rest? The poor man seems well bred… his table manners…"

"You poor dear…such a loving heart. Don't you understand about street people? He probably sleeps under bridges. Is kicked about by bullies who steal whatever he has. And I'd bet he has a prison record…"

"Please stop…let's move him to the…barn. I can't stand to look at…him…and think about…"

"Shush, dear. It's right. Believe me."

Together they lifted the frail man and carried him from the house and placed him in a wheel barrow that waited outside. Mort kissed his lovely wife and said, "You clean up inside, and I'll get started with our sleeping friend. He won't have to beg to survive from this day forward."

"From this day forward," she repeated, "sounds so pompous …like something an Episcopalian minister might say…at a wedding…I wonder if he's married"

He glanced back as he reached the barn. She stood in the doorway, a shapely silhouette against the light from the kitchen. He thought of embalming her beautiful body one day. His hands trembled as he unlocked the door to their personal mortuary.

9

The downtown park where they found him overlooks the Hillsborough River. Across the river, the silver Moorish towers on the University of Tampa's campus gleamed in the morning sun. Billy's embalmed corpse lay on a bench. His hands were folded on his thin chest, and a note was pinned to his clean Members Only jacket:

Mayor and Commissioners:

He called himself Billy, another of our society's failures. He's been given what our Mayor and Commissioners didn't give him—a meal, a bath, clean clothing, and peace. He will no longer be forced to stand on a street corner and beg for food. For your scraps. Shame. Shame.   The Mortician

"No I D?" Nan Delacorte asked the uniformed officer who had discovered the body.

"Haven't checked his pockets. Been waiting on you guys...and the crime scene crew."

"Your name?" I asked.

"Finney. Dan Finney."

"Okay, Dan. Why don't you get some crime scene tape and set up a perimeter...keep the early morning thrill seekers at bay." Officer Finney nodded and walked to his cruiser for a roll of the standard yellow tape used to mark off crime scenes.

Nan knelt beside the park bench and carefully went through Billy's pockets. Turned up nothing but some lint, which she bagged. Completing the task, she stood and shook her head. "Looks as though our kooky friends ran over him with a Hoover vacuum." The sound of a vehicle braking took her attention to where a white van had rolled to a stop. "Here comes Broadhurst's crew," she added, referring to the forensics team headed by Dr. Agnostic "Agnes" Broadhurst, department head.

"Wonder how he picked up a name like Agnostic?" Nan asked.

"You've never heard?"

"No. Tell...tell...before my curiosity overwhelms my self control and I pee myself."

"It goes like this. His mother wanted a girl. When it turned out to be a boy, she decided to tease his father...who refused to attend church with her. She entered Agnostic on the hospital registry and birth certificate. They had their laugh, but forgot to change the record. They called him Damon...which should have been the name on the records. When he signed up for the Marine Corp...Vietnam...he had to get a copy of his birth certificate from the office of vital statistics. There it was. Agnostic Broadhurst. He was so pissed, he refused to change it. His fellow travelers came up with the Agnes thing."

"That a true story?"

"It's the way he tells it."

"He must be nuts not changing it."

"Maybe idiosyncratic...but he knows what he's doing."

"Idiosyncratic? Odd would be better."

"Yeah. That'll work."

The ME's team got to the scene, and I left Nan to mark time while I returned to our unmarked car to call the Lieutenant.

* * *

I had just returned to my desk when I received the anticipated, but dreaded call from Midge. She said I should come home. It was mother, of course. She'd lapsed into a coma. I entered her bedroom with Midge twenty minutes after leaving the squad room. I was too late. My sweet Mother had passed away. The woman who'd nursed me, taken care of my hurts, loved me unequivocally, and taught me how to love was gone.

Dad was on his knees beside her bed. I joined him, putting an arm over his shoulders and adding my tears to his. I reached across the bed and took her hand. Still warm. There was a gentle smile on her lips. Like she knew something we didn't know. Beautiful in life, she was still beautiful in death. Our comforter in life. Who would comfort us now? I looked at Midge. She smiled and brushed my hair from my forehead. I took her hand and kissed it. Love carries us forward, I thought. As long as there's love, we can survive any tragedy. Dad would need love in bushels. He'd have ours but would ours be enough?

10

I returned to my desk four days after we buried Mom. Depressed didn't come close to describing my mood, but I felt a need to work. A need to forget or try to forget. Nan saw me come in and reached my desk before I did.

"You look like hell," she said, taking my hand and giving it a gentle squeeze. Nan didn't believe in hugs—at least not on company time.

"I'm not pretty anymore?" I said.

"If a wet bar towel is pretty, you're pretty."

I dropped into my chair. She sat on the corner of my desk. "You could grab a chair," I said.

"Sitting here gives me a chance to show my gams."

"Gams?" I said, frowning.

"Legs. Like in old gangster movies. Cagney. Robinson. Bogart. Raft. They all called legs gams."

"Before my time," I said, glancing at her gams. They were nice. Shapely—at least from mid-thigh down.

"You want to be a real tough cop, you'd better pick up some of the old but good videos. You know... Key Largo...Maltese Falcon. Get more bang for your buck."

"Not interested. I'm into James Bonds...all of them. So, small talk out of the way, let's talk about our case, shall we?"

Having done her best to cheer me up by showing me her "gams" and indulging in associated banter, she said, "Right," slipped off the corner of my desk, and went for a chair.

"So, what's gone down?" I asked when she returned. "We get an ID on our park bench mummy?"

"Our computer techs took a picture and dressed it up. Did five or six versions. Beard. Long hair. Short hair and short beard. The works. We posted them around and ran them as a grouping in the Tribune. So far, we've gotten a dozen responses...told five or six of the most promising we'd get in touch when you came in. Also heard from a pizza shop owner in Ybor City. Said he thought he recognized the guy as someone who panhandled at the I-4 exit at 22nd Street and took lunch in his shop. Says guy's name is Billy and... get this...says he saw him get into a car with a well-dressed dude he'd never seen in the area before. A total stranger."

"Does sound promising," I said. "You've got an address?"

"Certainly. You think I'd turn down a chance to scrounge a free pizza?"

"We're not supposed to take freebies."

"I'll trust you not to squeal."

"Don't. I'm a by-the- book guy," I said as we left the squad room and headed for Ybor city, an old section of Tampa a dozen or so blocks from the center of downtown.

* * *

We introduced ourselves to Anthony Rizzo, the owner of Tony's Pizza Place. Rizzo was an affable guy with a pizza pampered tummy, a big smile, and an absence of hair. His comb over didn't conceal a thing.

"Hey, you guys came like pretty damn quick after I called. What's up with Billy?"

"Billy's dead," I said.

"Dead? Gee. That's too bad. I'd better tell Georgia."

"Who's Georgia?" I asked.

"Georgia Selby. His landlady. Billy rents...rented...a second floor apartment from her. Place is only coupla' blocks away."

"Billy wasn't an itinerant...a drifter?"

"Drifter? Hell no. He's been around here as long as I can remember. Maybe ten years. Yeah, at least ten years."

I looked at Nan. She was smiling at Anthony. Begging. I got the message and thought I'd better take action before she barked. "Anthony, could you sit with us for a few minutes while I take some notes...and while my partner feeds her face. I think she's angling for a pizza with at least six toppings. Could that lovely lady behind the counter whip out a small pizza with the works? I'll pay."

"Lovely lady? Oh...you mean Angelica, my wife. You got it detective."

While Nan munched, I got around to turning on my recorder and questioning Anthony. First, I asked for directions to Miz Selby's place. I copied the directions and, after placing my note pad in an inside pocket, I started my interrogation.

"Now, tell me about what you saw. You told my partner that Billy got into a car with another man. Correct?"

"Sure did. The two of them came walking from Billy's corner to the car...a blue Ford Focus. It was parked in the corner parking lot across the street. Right over there." Rizzo pointed at a small paved lot.

"You're sure about that?"

"Damn sure. The guy sat there for maybe a half hour before he went to where Billy was."

"Was the guy tall, short, young, old?"

"Was maybe five-ten, Not over six foot. Built more like you than me," he said, laughed, and rubbed his belly.

"Built like your average guy? Sort of an average guy in appearance? Nothing stood out, right?"

"Yeah, average build. Not big shoulders like you, though." "Caucasian?" I continued, disregarding Nan's giggle following the "broad shoulders" comment.

"White? Yeah. Near as I could tell. You understand he was wearing a long sleeve jacket...dark blue or black...and gray pants and a blue ball cap that shaded his face."

"Special kind of ball cap?"

"Yeah...New York Yankee cap."

"You a Yankee fan?"

"Hell no. Red Sox."

"You didn't say whether he was young or old."

"Walked like he was young...in good shape. Long strides...no limp or nothing like that."

"Did it seem that he was forcing Billy to get into the car?"

"No way. I saw him pull money from his wallet. Looked like he paid Billy to go along."

"Approximately what time was this?"

"Let's see...One of my regulars came in...comes in about Seven-thirty most nights. Could have been a few minutes earlier."

"So they left around that time?"

"Right. Drove away about the time I went to take care of my regular."

"Bad deal for Billy," I said.

"You think the guy who picked him up killed him?" Angelo asked.

"A distinct possibility," I said, while thinking: Who else? Unless Mort's got himself a pick up and delivery service. "You didn't happen to pick up a license number...part of one maybe?"

"Like I said, I had to wait a table 'bout the time they drove off."

Part Two

Death: Once expressed in ceremony and tears, sorrow acquires space in the subconscious from which it may slither forth and compel moods that ravage one's faith and occasionally deplete one's desire to live.

CBW - 08

11

After Nan finished her pizza, dabbed up the crumbs with the tip of an index finger, and went to the restroom, we thanked Angelo and headed for Georgia Selby's place. It was as Angelo promised only a "coupla' blocks away." Unlike many old frame houses in the area, the house appeared to be well maintained. Freshly painted with petunia-filled flower boxes under each of its six front windows. The door bell was also in good working order. Two pushes and the door opened.

Georgia Selby was also freshly painted. A nicely-configured woman in her early forties with good teeth, manicured nails, and maybe a touch too much make-up. She had the appearance of a working girl who'd given up the trade before it gave up on her.

"Miss Selby?" Nan asked, showing her badge.

"Yes, I'm Georgia Selby. This is about Billy, isn't it?"

"Yes," Nan said. "Why did you think it would be about him?"

"No mystery. He hasn't been here for several days. He usually tells me if he's going away. If I'm at work, he leaves a note. Oh…and I saw the pictures in the Tribune…haven't had an opportunity to call."

"Where do you work, Ma'am?" I asked.

"I teach Computer Science at the community college branch here in Ybor."

This came as no surprise. After listening to her speak, I had revised my assessment. I knew she wasn't your every day retired lady of the night.

"Could we come in, Ma'am?" Ma'am? I wondered if I were beginning to sound like Joe Friday. A laconic character I knew from TV re-runs.

"Yes, of course. And, please, it's Georgia. Ma'am makes it sound as though I'm out of circulation."

"You're not married?" Nan asked.

"No, not at the moment. But I'm hunting." She looked at me and asked, "Are you available, Detective?"

Her eyes smiled. I'd seen her scan my left hand. She knew.

"Yes, damn it," I said. Nan laughed and so did Georgia. In our business it was nice to meet gracious, fun people. Those on our beat are usually so deep in anguish and anger they've forgotten how to laugh—or to smile.

"How long have you known Billy and does he have a last name?" It was Nan's turn to ask questions. My turn to observe. My recorder was on. Had been on.

"He's rented from me for seven years...ever since I bought the place. His name? His social security checks came in the name of William Rockefeller."

"Rockefeller? No lie?"

"No lie. He showed me his check one day. It was for the maximum amount."

"Why in the hell...excuse me…why was he panhandling?"

"Told me it helped pass time and helped subsidize his hobby."

"What hobby?" Now I was really curious.

"Coin collecting. He has a superb collection. Would you like to see his apartment?"

"Sure would," Nan and I said in unison.

Ten steps to a second floor landing led us to the late William "Billy" Rockefeller's apartment door. Georgia unlocked the door and preceded us into the apartment. It was clean, airy and bright. The four room layout included a kitchenette, a master bedroom with bath, living room, and a second bedroom that housed his hobby.

A workbench that I assumed he used to clean and mount his collection sat beneath a small window. Spaced along two interior walls were six shelving units. Each units' four, felt-covered shelves displayed Billy's collection.

"My God," I said. "It must be worth thousands."

"Ten million," Georgia said. "That's what he told me the last time he had it appraised...two years ago."

"Dollars?"

"Yes. Dollars." Georgia said with a pleasant smile.

"He was a millionaire? A multi-millionaire?" Nan managed to open her jaw, which had been temporarily locked by shock and awe.

"I wonder who will inherit all of this?" I asked, waving a hand in the direction of the shelves. I don't think I was a damned bit surprised by the answer.

"I will," Georgia said. "I have a copy of the will downstairs. The original is in a lock box in Billy's bedroom closet...along with several dozen bearer bonds. Would you like to see the will?"

"I certainly would," I said.

"He didn't mention a detective named Delacorte in his will did he?" Nan asked.

"No, dear, he didn't. Sorry."

"It's okay...just thought I'd ask."

* * *

Nan and I remained silent until we were within sight of the station. I suppose we were still recovering from finding that Mort and Marian's latest victim had millions.

"Quite a surprise?" I said.

"Damned nice surprise for Georgia Selby. All good things come to him...or her...who waits. Or is it to he or she who waits?"

"Take your choice," I said. "Georgia wasn't surprised, though." "Not a bit...since she knew it was coming some day. Almost enough money to kill for... if one were so inclined."

"You suggesting she killed Billy boy...or had him put down?"

"Not unless she's a mortician on the side," Nan said.

"Perhaps she knows one."

"There's a thought," Nan said.

I pulled into our parking slot and set the brake. "You know...Mort and Marian have advertised the virtue of helping poor unfortunates escape to the hereafter. Wonder how they'd react if they found out that their first victim had half a million coming and that the second could have bought the Skyway Bridge."

"Might compel them to do better research...slow them down some," Nan said then continued, "You know...listening to the pizza man...Anthony...I realized that we can cross the Parnell's off our suspect list."

"You sure of that?"

"Hell yes. Angelo said the guy that picked Billy up was like a max of six feet. Parnell is at least six five... maybe six-six...tall and thin."

"The Parnell's have a son who matches Angelo's description," I said.

"You don't believe...sure…it's a possibility. A family of morticians who have a great fondness for macabre family entertainment."

"Give you another thought to chew on," I said.

"Yeah?"

"What if Georgia Selby and the Parnells are acquainted?"

"Now there's a thought worth putting one's molars to."

"How about one's brain?"

"Wise ass," Nan said with a grin.

* * *

Sheila was waiting for me when we walked into the reception area of the squad room. "Woman named Victoria Caruso called. Asked that you call back as soon as you came in. Said you know the number."

"Thanks, Sheila," I said.

"Who's Victoria Caruso? A playmate?" Nan asked.

"I don't play off the home field these days. Victoria's the sweet kid I rescued from that bastard Sampson... you know, guy who organized the rape of April Perry. She works for my Dad now...in his office." I wasn't in the mood for kidding. Nan got it. She left to give me some space when we reached my desk.

My conversation with Victoria was brief. I hung up and went to where Nan was standing. "I've got to go home, kid. When the Lieutenant gets back from lunch, would you fill him in on what we learned about Billy. Here's the number where he can reach me...just in case." I departed with that, leaving her with a lot of unanswered questions and a Post-It note dangling between the thumb and index finger of her right hand.

12

Twenty minutes later, I reached the office of Paxton Construction, Inc. Midge was sitting with Victoria Caruso and Mary Jane Stiffler at the only table in the office lunch room. Victoria and Mary Jane were the only full time staff members in the office. Mary Jane—a hard fifty—knew the business well enough to take on day-to-day things with little or no directions from Dad.

"What's up, guys?" I kissed Midge and took a fourth chair at the table.

"Have a sandwich," Midge said. "I made them from your mom's ham salad recipe." Midge knew the way to my heart from any point on the compass. Mom's ham salad was made with bologna. It was delicious.

I took a half sandwich and held it. "Why am I here?" I asked Victoria.

"It's your Dad."

"What about him.? Where the hell is he?" I put the half sandwich back on the plate.

"We're not certain," Mary Jane broke in. "He hasn't been here since the funeral...not here in the office, anyway."

"His car's always here when I get home."

"Midge says he's been returning home around five. Goes directly into the house...and locks the door. He doesn't answer telephone calls...or the door bell."

"Midge. Why didn't you tell me?"

"The first three days...we thought he was just going somewhere to get away...the beach maybe...couldn't bear being around the house without your Mom. Yesterday, I watched for him...saw him come in and..." she hesitated.

"And what, for God's sake?" I said, grabbing her arm.

"He...was drunk. Very drunk. He was having trouble unlocking the door. I went to help him, and he pushed me away...with an expletive."

"Drunk.? Pushed you away? That's not Dad." I took Midge's hand and kissed it by way of apology for him. She smiled and all was right with the world. Almost.

After several minutes of silence, "I said, "Do you guys have any idea where he would go to drink?"

Victoria shook her head. Mary Jane picked up the slack and said, "There's a small restaurant bar on Route 92...The Back Trail Bar and Grille...where he used to take his foremen when they finished a big job. Bought them dinner and a few drinks. Only time I knew him to drink was then."

I stood. We all knew where I was going. "I'll find him, Mary Jane. By the way how are things going with the job schedule?"

"No problems we can't handle right now. We've got good crews, and they all have a full load...but your Dad...he's the one customer's want to talk to. He's the one who keeps the jobs coming."

"But things are okay for the time being?"

"Yes...but we worry. The guys are beginning to wonder where he is. Why he's not out checking the jobs."

"I know," I said. I kissed Midge again and left the office for the Back Trail Bar and Grille.

* * *

I found Dad at the Back Trail Bar and Grille. It was a little after two in the afternoon, a slow time for such back road establishments. Dad was one of three people in the barroom section; the other two, the bartender and a marginally mobile waitress. The kind of tired lady that you feel sorry for because you know she must work to survive. You know that the work is too hard. You know her feet hurt. Her back aches. I felt like tipping her and I hadn't even had a drink. I put five dollars in her apron pocket and told her to buy a pack of Wrigleys.

Dad was at the bar nursing a half-empty cocktail glass. Something on the rocks. I sat beside him The stool was wobbly. I exchanged it for another.

"Hello, Dad. How about buying me a drink?"

He didn't look up from the rim of the glass. "You don't drink," he said.

"I could start."

"What the hell for?"

"Maybe for the same reason you're getting soused every day. I miss Mom, too."

"You got Midge. I've got nothing...now. Damn cancer took away everything I worked my ass off for thirty years."

"I could feel insulted by that remark. You still have me...for what that's worth. And Midge loves you like the father she lost some time ago. And...let's see... you've got a grandchild on the way. You've got a construction company with a great reputation and a few dozen families who depend on you being there for them. Sixty or seventy men, women, and children who think you're a great guy. You going to tell them they're wrong? That you're a washed up old bastard..."

He wheeled around on his bar stool, his eyes full of anguish. He lifted a massive fist and took a wild swing that grazed my chin. "Want another shot, Dad? I've got time if you've got the need."

Instead of swinging again, he put his arms around me and began to sob. "I know, son. I know. I've been a total ass...acting in ways Mom wouldn't have wanted... disgracing her memory by forgetting you...the others that she loved so much. But I miss her so...damned house is so damned empty. She had ways of making me feel admired...loved. Oh, dear God, why? I know you loved her, too. Why take her? Why not me?"

I held him for a minute before asking, "You ready to go home to those other people who love you as much as I do. And...if it would help...I'll ask Midge if she'd be willing for us to move in with you and start filling those big empty spaces with adorable little urchins."

He released his bear hug, wiped his face on his sleeve and asked, "You would? You and Midge would move in with me?" A small smile emerged with the question.

"Probably, since the mighty one has already suggested it several times."

We walked from the Back Trail Bar and Grille. His arm was over my shoulder. We emerged from the bar room catharsis with our love, our hopes and dreams reinvigorated. Intact and unblemished. I'd never look back in sorrow, but with the knowledge that the beautiful creature who had made our lives so complete was still with us. If that sounds mawkish to the reader, it may because in your life you have never experienced a love by someone like Mom. I felt healed. I wasn't too certain about Dad. He wouldn't heal so easily.

13

I returned to the precinct after an emotional scene of hugging, kissing, apologies, and tearful acceptances of apologies. When I left his office, Dad was guzzling black coffee and he and Midge were locked up in a discussion of our pending move to the "big" house. I joined Nan at her desk and gave her the reason for my unexplained departure—without getting into the emotional stuff.

"Glad things worked out, Rock. Must be very hard to lose someone who's that important to you."

"Yeah. Very difficult," I said. And that was that.

"I had some thoughts about our case while you were out bar hopping," Nan said, flipping open a spiral note pad.

"Let's hear it."

"I thought over what you said about a tie between the Parnells and Georgia Selby. I think it's a probability…not a possibility."

"Go on."

"I also agree that Victor Parnell could be the tie that binds."

"So?"

"Since I agree with you on both counts, I believe we should take a good look at Victor. Find out what he does for fun."

"That it? So far I find myself agreeing with me."

"One more thing. The hit on Mary O'Malley could have been to throw us off track when they took out Billy Rockefeller."

"You're starting to think like a criminal, partner."

"Thanks. I've heard that's what makes a good detective."

"But we're left with the alternative that Mort and Marian are two kooks who honestly believe they are performing a humane service and killed Mary and Billy to end their suffering."

"And if the alternative is true, there should be another embalmed cadaver in our near future?"

"We'll have to consider both angles. Billy boy an act of misguided compassion or an effort to transfer

Billy's bucks from his pockets to Georgia and a male friend's...who's also a mortician."

"You've been thinking, too," Nan said.

"Yup. I've got one other idea. I'd like to hear your reaction."

"Shoot, partner. I'm all ears."

"I hadn't noticed," I said.

"Why do you think I wear my hair the way I do."

"Female duplicity," I said. Then I told her my idea.

* * *

Marian turned to Mort who was reading a Patterson novel and sipping a Scotch on the rocks. "My God, did you hear that?"

"What, sweets?" He closed the book, marking his place with his free index finger.

"That panhandler...Billy...he had a fortune in rare coins and bearer bonds. We didn't euthanize a destitute person...he was a wealthy man. We did something horrible." She turned off the TV, stood, and began to pace.

"Sad. But he did present himself as a panhandling bum." Mort downed his drink and placed the empty glass on a side table.

"Panhandling bum. You sound so damned callous. How can you treat what we did with such indifference now that you know he was wealthy?"

"We erred...we made a mistake...but our motives, our intentions were chaste. We were tricked by his beggar's façade. So, he brought his elimination on himself."

"Chaste? And what about Mary O'Malley?"

He frowned. "What about Mary O'Malley?"

"She was due to receive a half million from an insurance policy, a fact that was also in the news report."

He rose and confronted her. Attempted to take her into his arms. She pushed him away. "Don't you see what they're doing?" he said.

"What who is doing?"

"The police. They must be planting these stories."

"And why would they do that?"

"To force us to discontinue our work...our mission. Do you honestly believe that hairy little creature...who gorged himself on your beans and ribs...that creature was a multi-millionaire?"

"Hairy little creature? You don't sound like a man who believes he's doing God's work by euthanizing destitute, suffering people."

"And what do I sound like, dear?"

"You sound like...like...a murderer. Like someone who enjoys killing."

"How can you infer such a thing, say such a thing after all we've been to each other? After all we've shared."

"I can say it...because it's what I feel."

"Really. One thing you must realize, sweetheart. If I'm a murderer, what are you?" His handsome face was suddenly ugly, lips twisted into a grotesque smirk. His narrowed eyes were menacing, demonic. Fright gripped her. She suddenly realized that this man she had pledged to love, honor, and obey was evil.

"Shall we go to bed, dear," he said as he took her hand in a firm grip. She felt resistance could be fatal. Trembling, she allowed him to lead her to the bedroom and to whatever would follow.

* * *

Victor Parnell didn't seem like a criminal. His features were somewhat feminine: pug nose, small ears tight to the skull, dimpled cheeks, and wavy blond hair. He had a slender build, and stood about five ten. He greeted Nan and me in the crematorium office with a gracious smile. I'd seen that smile on the benign faces of a few dozen funeral home attendants during my adult life. He obviously knew more about the business than just burning bodies.

He directed us to a grouping of plush furniture in one corner of his spacious office. "My father called. Said you guys were at his place and asked about me. Said you'd be stopping by. Before you begin asking your questions, could I offer you something?" He gestured toward a small wet bar across the room.

"No thanks. Drinking on the job's against department policy," I said. My quick, firm response was a pre-emptive strike, knowing Nan's penchant for an occasional bourbon on the rocks. And as I've suggested previously, Nan is a free spirit with a loathing of any regulations she considers stupid, which includes most of them.

"Okay. How may I help you, Detectives?"

"We're...as I suppose you've heard...investigating two recent murders by person or persons with a professional mortician's training."

"Yes, I'm aware of that. And I know you had my parents verify the skill of the person...or persons...who killed those poor people."

"How long have you been in the business, Mister Parnell," Nan asked. I noticed she was flashing her gams.

"Well...I graduated from Samuelson in 1998. So ten years. I worked in the funeral home for five years before I took over here. Former manager passed away... wonderful man...an uncle."

"Do you consider yourself a fully competent mortician?"

"I don't know what fully competent means. I'm well trained and conscientious. Is that what you're asking?"

"Yes. That's fine. Have you ever taken any coursework at the community college branch in Ybor City?" I asked.

His white face got whiter. "Well...let's see. I'm sort of a professional student. I like to learn new things, you know."

"Like data processing...computer science?"

"Why yes...I did take a course there. Uh...two maybe three years ago."

"We will check, Mister Parnell. It's not overly important, but we like to be accurate," Nan said.

"Of course. As I think about it...it was the winter term last year. That would make it fifteen months ago. Such things are easy to forget, you know...when one has so much going on."

"We understand," I said. "Who was your instructor for the course?"

"Damn...it's so hard...to..."

"Was it Georgia Selby?" Nan asked.

"Yes...that's who it was. I'd completely forgotten."

"We've heard that you and Professor Selby were rather chummy," I said. It was a lie to the extent that we hadn't heard a damned thing about their relationship. But it helped. He was wilting like a shirt collar with too little starch on a July afternoon.

Slumping in his chair, he said, "Okay. Georgia and I had something going after class."

"For the whole term?" Nan asked.

"Yes."

"A sexual relationship?"

"Yes."

"Still going on?" I asked.

He perked up. "Hell no. She picked up another guy...the very next term. Look, Detectives, I'm happily married. Have a wonderful wife. Sheri. Dr. Dustan Samuelson's daughter. So, if I seemed somewhat devious..."

"Somewhat?" Nan said.

"Okay. I tried to hold back. You understand?"

"Most certainly, since you're so happily married," I said. "I think we're finished for now. We may get back to you after we talk to Miss Selby again."

"Is that necessary? It's over, you know."

"It's necessary," I said. "You like baseball, Victor?"

"Why?"

"I've got tickets to the Red Sox series with the Rays next week. You interested?"

"Hell no. I'm a Yankee fan."

"Okay. I'll unload them back in the squad room." We stood and shook hands.

"Oh, I almost forgot,"

"Yes."

"Where were you last Thursday around dusk? Somewhere between six and seven?"

"Last Thursday between six and seven? Uh...let me check my calendar." Victor's face paled. He'd have been invisible on a bed sheet. Yes...I recall. I had a pick up."

"At the funeral home? Your folks place?"

"Yes."

"We'll verify that, you know."

"I have nothing to hide."

We left Victor at his wet bar with a bottle of Glenfiddich in his hand and his eyes on the telephone.

As we got into our vehicle, Nan said, "What if he'd been a Red Sox fan. You don't have any damned tickets."

"You didn't notice? He had a signed and framed picture of Derek Jeter on the wall behind his desk."

"Who?"

"The New York Yankee's all-pro shortstop."

"You're so smart."

"Either that or you don't know crap about baseball."

"Guilty as charged," Nan confessed as we left the crematorium behind. Then she added, "Ask me something about bourbons. Go ahead. Ask me."

14

Seeking escape from the previous night's encounter with her husband, Marian had arisen early and gone to the pet cemetery at the rear of the property. Now, kneeling beside a bed of multi-colored impatiens at the entrance, she plucked a few remaining weeds, dropped them into a bucket, and stood with a hand on her back.

She hadn't slept well. The truth about Mary O'Malley and Billy Rockefeller's financial status had been very disturbing to her. More disturbing was the way Mort had taken the news. He'd shown no remorse and treated the executions as lessons learned: "We'll have to check the finances of our candidates more carefully," he'd said and smiled.

After dumping the bucket of weeds on a compost pile outside the entrance, she locked the gate, climbed aboard a garden tractor, and headed back to the house.

Marian knew that their relationship could never be the same. To her horror, she'd discovered a side of him she hadn't seen before. The pity, the desire to help stray animals—the thing that had brought them together—that compassion was hers alone. She knew now it had been manufactured, a pretense to win her love. He was a consummate actor. Even the tears she had seen him shed over a cadaver—she now believed—were manufactured. If anything, they were tears derived from the pleasure of taking a life. The tears of a sadistic monster.

One other thing she knew for certain. He would not allow her to leave him. She knew that he would keep her with him one way or another. On a slab if necessary. She shuddered and tears dimmed her lovely eyes.

* * *

Nan and I called it a day after leaving Victor Parnell. We believed Victor would clear his alibi with his parents before we'd left the crematorium parking lot. So we decided to check it out the next day. Get the name of the cadaver and the time of the pick up. We'd also decided to add a second visit with Georgia Selby to the next day's agenda. When I arrived home—a trifle early—I found Dad directing a move from our house to his place. A shaker and mover, Dad had assigned two of his construction crews to the task of moving the major items. Mary Jane, Victoria, and three part-time women –the office crew—were assisting in the placement of furniture and décor items under Midge's direction.

Coming to where I stood, Midge crawled up my frame and kissed me hard. "You're early," she said.

"Your condition...uh...should you be doing this?"

"Silly. I'm not going to hurt a three month fetus by moving my lips."

I held her and kissed her again. "I need a shower. Are there still towels in our place?" I asked, nodding toward what was rapidly becoming our former residence on a half-acre lot next door.

"Yup. Soap, towels, and shampoo...and just in case...why don't you shave."

"Just in case of what?" I said.

"You know...you brute," she said with a wicked grin on her face as she went back to work.

I stood smiling at her bouncy little butt as she walked away. I was on my way to the shower when the phone rang.

"Hello...Rock Paxton here."

"Are you...the detective who's involved with the Mary O'Malley murder?" the female caller asked.

"Yes...who is this?"

"I'm the wife of...oh my God. What are you..." With that, the phone went dead. I rang the operator and identified myself. I was connected to a supervisor and gave her the number that had popped up on my caller ID. After a several minutes, my inquiry was answered. "Listing is for the Samuelson College of Mortuary Science. Is there anything else, Officer Paxton?"

"No," I said. I called Nan and waited impatiently until she answered. "What in the hell are you doing?" I asked.

"Wouldn't you like to know," she said.

"Probably something disgusting," I said. Then I told her about the call from the college and asked her to meet me there. She didn't sound too happy about it.

"You know something," she said.

"I know a little bit about a lot of things...what's the problem?"

"This job sucks," she said.

"Tell me about it," I said, thinking about the lascivious smile Midge had laid on me before walking away.

* * *

Sobbing, her eyes swollen and red, Marian looked up from the floor where he'd thrown her. "I swear I was calling Jenny Dixon…to see if she wanted to go shopping Saturday. Honestly. Please believe me. That's all it was."

"I didn't hear you use the word 'detective' in your conversation with your dear friend?"

"I…I was having difficulty hearing her…I said something about her phone being defective. That could have been what you heard."

He stared at her. "Why don't you call Jennifer, now. Tell her you ended the conversation because the cat got on the dinner table…or something like that. Remember. I'll be right beside you, darling."

15

Dr. Dustan Samuelson was as genial as a mama lion on a nocturnal hunt, and his pale blue eyes looked as though they'd spent the day in deep freeze. He ignored my outstretched hand and stared at Nan as though she were a cod on ice rather than a rather attractive young woman with nice gams.

"I don't understand why this visit couldn't have waited until tomorrow, Mr. Payton."

"Detective Paxton."

"All right. Detective Paxton. Whatever pleases you. Our evening classes are about to begin, and most of our clerical staff have left for the day. So....?"

"I received a call from a phone listed to your college, Doctor. The call was from a very frightened woman... a young woman...who hung up before I could get a name. I got the impression she was forced to discontinue the call. She may have been in danger."

"We have several listings. Most are cordless phones. We also have several cell phones we check out to staff members who must make business calls when they're off the campus."

I handed him a Post-it slip with the number scrawled on it. "This is the number, Doctor. Do you have any idea who might have access to it?"

"I'm not the office manager, Detective. I'm the founder and president of this institution," he said. "Perhaps in your position you're charged with keeping track of minutiae. I employ people to take care of minor operational details."

His haughty response ticked me off. "Okay…Mister Samuelson …we'll come back tomorrow and talk to the peasants who clean up your..."

"Doctor...would you mind showing us around?" Nan interrupted, obviously believing that I was about to say something nasty, which I was. "We know someone using one of your phones was in danger, and we need to nose around and make certain she isn't here. If you'd be so kind." She leaned forward, arching her back and batting her eyes.

"Well...we're very proud of our facility. I'd be happy to take you around. Uh...what is your name, dear?"

"Detective Nan Delacorte, Doctor. Please call me Nan." She took his arm and walked toward the central lobby. I followed behind. I'd never thought of a Nan as a woman capable of exercising her feminine wiles. But she'd certainly beguiled the hell out of Doctor Samuelson who appeared to have some vulnerability to feminine charm and prominent physical attributes after all..

* * *

We completed our guided tour of the College and arrived in the foyer. Dr. Samuelson—who'd taken a fancy to my partner—shook Nan's hand and ignored mine. This didn't bother me when I visualized the things his hands had probably touched that very day.

"Dad...when you're finished...could you give me a few minutes?"

I turned to encounter the biggest, brightest, brown eyes I'd ever seen. The eyes were accompanied by full lips, high cheekbones, shining black hair and a dimpled chin. Then, there was her body. I won't go into specific details of her physique since Midge may read this record of our investigation if I do a Wambaugh and have it published.

"Detectives. This is my daughter, Dr. Sheri Samuelson, a professor of anatomy here."

"A pleasure, Doctor," I said. Extending my hand. Her hand was very warm in contrast to her father's.

"You're detectives?" I detected a quiver in her soft, throaty voice.

"Yes. We're investigating a call from a cell phone listing for the college. The call was from a young woman who seemed rather desperate."

"Oh, I see." Her eyes turned to her father. "I'll get with you later, Dad."

"Before you go, Dr. Samuelson, can we assume that you don't know who might have placed the call?" Nan asked.

"No...I have no idea."

"I assume that you're not married, Doctor." I knew she was, but it was a conversation starter.

She glanced at her father before responding. "Well... yes...I am married."

"You use your maiden name because...?"

"I use it for several reasons."

"Such as?"

"I worked for the college prior to getting married. I'm very active in the community, and Dad and I felt retaining the family name helped the college...you know, because of my credentials and such."

"What sort of community activities are..."

"I resent this inquisition," Dustan interrupted. "My daughter has nothing to do with your investigation."

"I...don't mind, Dad. My activities...I'm a member of the Humane Society. I'm also an adjunct .professor of biology at the University of Tampa."

"You are busy," I said and added, "Doesn't your husband mind?"

"Some."

"What is his name...your husbands?" Nan asked.

"Victor," she said.

"Victor Parnell?"

"Yes. Victor's my husband." Dr. Sheri Samuelson Parnell sounded as though she wanted to cry.

"What a coincidence," I said.

"In what way?" she said.

"We interviewed your husband today in connection with two murders."

"Two murders?" Sheri Samuelson Parnell leaned against her father's chest.

"Yes," I said. "Perhaps you've read the newspaper accounts. They're being call The Mortician Murders."

"Are you ill, dear?" Dr. Dustan asked daughter Sheri.

* * *

"It was eight o'clock when I arrived home Midge was waiting for me at the side door of our new home. The move was complete and she appeared to be exhausted. Despite that, her greeting was as hearty as ever

"I...thought   you'd...never...get...back.   Was...it worth...the time?" she said, her words interspersed by a series of very warm kisses. I stopped thinking about Sheri Samuelson Parnell and started thinking about a hot shower, dinner, and what would most probably follow if I read the signals correctly.

16

Georgia Selby didn't seem surprised by our return visit or by Nan's first question after we sat down together at her kitchen table. "Did you have an affair with Victor Parnell?"

"Oh, yes, since you ask. I had a delightful interlude with Victor. He's a very sweet boy. A marvelous lover, considering his youth and relative inexperience."

"During this interlude, did you know he was a married man?"

"Yes. I knew. I had the feeling he wanted to experiment with a more mature woman. I believe he found it...uh...profitable."

"Do you know who his wife is?" I asked.

"Yes...her name was on his registration form as the person to call in the event of an emergency. I understand she's a very lovely young woman."

"Very," I said. "You don't seem surprised that we're back."

"Simple logic said you would be. Billy was murdered by someone who calls himself the Mortician. I was Billy's landlady, and I had a fling with a mortician, ergo, another visit from two very charming and clever detectives."

"You left out a very important factor in your chain of logic."

"Yes?"

"Come on, Ms. Selby. It was no accident...leaving out the most important fact."

"I suppose you're referring to motive...the matter of Billy's will...the wonderful fortune the dear man left me."

"You got it," I said.

"So, you suspect I may have colluded with Victor to murder Billy for his money?"

"Makes sense, doesn't it. Victor embalms Billy and you two share the estate after probate and taxes."

"I'm sure that it makes sense to you...to anyone who's paid to be suspicious. But I had nothing to do with the murder...and I imagine Victor has a very solid alibi...he's a very busy young man, you know."

"Did he tell you he would arrange a very good alibi?"

"No he didn't. Why should he since neither of us had anything to do with Billy's death? May I ask... since you must have talked to him to learn about our relationship...did he have an acceptable alibi?"

"Depends on what you'd call acceptable. It wasn't what we'd consider air tight, but we're checking. We've got a few things to look into before we reach a decision on you two and your little interlude. I should warn you that play time is over, Ms. Selby. If you've withheld anything...if you have something to share with us... the sooner the better. We will put the pieces together eventually."

Her response was subdued. "I'm sure you will, Detective Paxton. You're so utterly clever. So...is that it? If it is, I have a class in exactly twenty minutes. You may check if you like." She stood and we did likewise. She led us to the door, opened it, gave us time to clear the sill, and slammed it behind us. I checked my right hip pocket to see if my wallet was still there. It was.

Our relationship with Ms. Georgia Selby had soured appreciably. And I had mixed feelings after leaving the immaculate house with its six window boxes full of bright-colored petunias.

"I don't think we'll be invited to her Christmas party, partner," I said.

"Damn. And I was so looking forward to tasting her bonbons."

"No comment on the bonbons thing, partner."

"I thought I could trap you into some lewd conversation. You're such a Boy Scout...absolutely no fun at all."

"What do you think, Nan? You pick up on anything with Selby?"

"I don't think we learned anything that we didn't already know," Nan said.

"We sure as hell didn't catch her with her bloomers down...to coin a phrase."

"Catch her with her bloomers down? To coin a phrase? Good lord. That was trite when Shakespeare was writing soliloquies."

"I know. I'm weak on current metaphors. Seriously, partner...I don't think we laid a glove...okay...I won't finish it. Another trite metaphor. Right?"

"Right. One thing's for certain, Rock. You've lost your touch, She didn't bat her big browns at you once," Nan said.

"I know I turned her off. I'm practicing to be a tough cop...like those guys who call legs 'gams'."

* * *

We walked from Georgia Selby's house to Tony's Pizza Place. Our purpose was to solicit Tony's help with a line up. See if he could pick Victor Parnell—the Yankee fan—from a line up of cops, mostly Tampa Bay fans. I had my hand on the door handle when Nan asked, "Should we arrange taps on Georgia and Victor's phones?"

"The Lieutenant's working on it," I said.

"If she's involved, she's probably already checking with Victor."

"Or with a lawyer."

"Or with both," Nan said, adding, "You don't suppose you could spring for another pizza...since we're in the neighborhood."

"I'll buy if you explain why I should."

"To keep your partner's tummy happy. You wouldn't want it growling ferociously at you all the way back to the squad room, would you?"

* * *

Mort was in the Volvo waiting when Marian walked from the internist's office. Since their confrontation over the O'Malley and Rockefeller fiascos, and her cell phone conversation with Jenny Dixon, she'd been nervous as hell and very cold in her response to his advances. He knew he'd lost the control over her that he'd gained by catering to her obsession with animals. That loss of control was a fact that made him extremely nervous, too.

"Hello, darling," he said, leaning toward her and kissing her cheek as she dropped into the passenger seat.

"Hello. Did you have a good day?" she asked.

"The normal...what did Doc Herman say?"

"Nothing I didn't expect. Gave me some sleep aids... samples ...and told me to lay off the coffee."

As he pulled away from the curb, he placed his right hand on her thigh. He felt her stiffen. He fought an angry reaction. "Touchy dear? You've been very distant since our little spat over...well...you know."

"Little spat?" Her voice trembled with repressed anger. "I can't believe you could kill two people...two individuals who had every reason to live...with such heartless disregard for what you'd done."

"What we'd done, dear. As I recall, you were a very willing participant."

"Willing because I believed you...believed in you."

"I've lost your trust? And your love? "She didn't respond so he continued. "If true, it could have tragic consequences. Without your love and trust, I have no control over what you might do."

"What I might do?"

"Yes. You might feel obligated to go to the police. I couldn't tolerate that. I would be forced to..."

"Are you threatening me?"

"No, not exactly. I'm trying to forge a revised understanding between us."

"A revised understanding? You know I can't go to the police. I have no desire to spend the rest of my life in prison."

"Yes. I needed you to say that."

"But there is something you need to understand, dear," Marian said.

"What's that?"

"Intercourse is out without my permission for the foreseeable future. Any time you come to my bed without permission, you will have to rape me...as you did the last time."

"Your bed?"

"Yes. I'll be sleeping in the spare bedroom from this night on. With the door locked and bolted."

17

"We couldn't find a judge who'd authorize wire taps on Victor Parnell and Georgia Selby's phones. Can't complain. We don't have much to justify taps."

I looked at Nan and we both nodded. "To be honest, Lieutenant, neither Nan or I thought it would happen. We checked Selby's teaching schedule for the night Mary O'Malley was picked up by Marian..."

"Who's Marian?" Agosto asked.

"That's the name Nan and I gave the Mortician's accomplice. Marian Knight was the name on the phony business card she gave O'Malley. We thought Mort and Marian worked better conversationally than he and she. Perp and perpess."

"La-de-da...conversationally. You been taking night classes in the vernacular, Rock?"

"Not exactly. I've been teaching a Spanish dude to speak English. He's a quick learner. It's tough to keep ahead of him."

"Good comeback, partner," Agosto said. "So, anything new that isn't on your reports?"

"You heard that we asked Parnell to appear in a line up. First thing he did was lawyer up. His lawyer advised him to go along."

"And...?"

"We put him and four other men in the line up. Rizzo picked out two possibles...based on build...one was Parnell. Said he couldn't be sure because a friggin' Yankee ball cap shaded the face of the guy who picked up Rockefeller."

"Friggin' Yankee cap? How could he?"

"Boston fan."

"Oh. That explains the sacrilege. Those bean town bums have no respect." Agosto paused, smiled, and said, "Okay, where are we?"

"Nan and I have three people...maybe four...to interview before narrowing our suspect list again."

"Names?"

"Dustan Samuelson, Jr., a licensed playboy and Peter and Adrianna Comstock. She owns and operates The Loving Shepherd Cemetery and Mortuary.

He's a CPA when he isn't helping his lovely wife do cadavers."

"You still believe your killer is among those on your original suspect list?"

"Speaking for myself...yes," I said.

"You agree with your partner, Detective Delacorte?"

"Yes sir. We devoted a lot of time doing background checks, financials, etceteras. I'll bet my...uh...next nose job that the killers are in that mix."

"By the way, of your current suspects, any agreed to a polygraph session yet?"

"Georgia Selby has...and we're setting it up...of course she wasn't on our original list."

"Okay. Keep me informed. Hey, Rock. I heard you're going to be a papa."

"You heard right, Lieutenant."

"My, my...will wonders never cease. Congratulations to you and Midge. I'm willing to be a Godfather... don't forget it."

* * *

When we reached our unmarked vehicle, I leaned on the top and looked across at Nan who was ready to slide into the driver's seat. "I didn't know you'd had a nose job."

"I wouldn't think of it. You wouldn't want me to utter a vulgarity in the Lieutenant's presence would you?"

"Of course not."

"So...I chose to say nose job rather than boob job... even though my nose could be described as patrician just as it is."

"Patrician? What's patrician?"

"Aristocratic, noble, upper class. Take a look." She turned sideways to display her profile. "What do you think?" she asked.

"I'd say it was perky. Cute," I said.

"That'll do," she said. We got into the modified Chevy Malibu. Nan started the engine and asked, "Where to first, partner?"

"Let's drop in on the Loving Shepherd Cemetery... see if there are any vacancies."

18

We arrived at the Loving Shepherd Funeral Home, which was situated on the front acre or so of the Loving Shepherd Cemetery. The building itself was a small rendering of an ante bellum landowner's residence.

Upon entering the building, we were greeted by a wisp of a man wearing a black suit, tie, black shoes and a white shirt. His sparse white hair was combed straight back. His smile was pleasant.

"May I assist you folks?"

"Are you Peter Cromwell?" I asked.

"Oh, no. I'm Dan Shepherd, Adrianna's uncle…her father's brother. Peter's at his office on Busch Boulevard. I can give you his address."

"Later, thanks. Is Ms. Cromwell in?"

"Yes. She's in her office. I'll check to see if she's free. Whom should I say...?"

"Detectives Paxton and Delacorte, Tampa Police Department,"

I said, flashing my badge.

"Oh, you're detectives." He walked to a small desk centered in the far end of the spacious foyer. He reached his niece through an intercom and returned smiling as though we were paying customers. "Adrianna is available. Follow me, please."

Adrianna Cromwell met us at the door. She had the shape and stature of a Las Vegas showgirl, ash blond hair, very blue eyes, and an oval face replete with dimples. I could visualize her doing many, many things other than embalming cadavers.

"Detectives Paxton and Delacorte," She said and smiled. "And who's who?"

"I'm Paxton, I said.

"I'm the other guy," Nan said, always the odd ball.

"Please come in and have a chair." There were two chairs in front of her desk. I allowed Nan first choice, gentleman that I am.

"Thanks for seeing us without notice, Ms. Cromwell. We don't like to surprise people," I said. The latter statement was, of course, a lie. Surprising a suspect could often be very profitable.

"I don't mind, Detective Paxton. Please, how may I help you?" She began toying with a jade locket.

"Have you heard about the Mortician murders?" Nan asked.

"Yes. Horrible. Two individuals murdered and embalmed. Hardly the act of a professional mortician."

"To the contrary. We're absolutely certain that the killer is a professional mortician."

"That's so hard to believe."

"We've had it confirmed by several experts in mortuary science," I said. So what, I thought, two could be several, and perhaps the Parnell's weren't exactly experts.

"That's shocking," Adrianna said. She'd stopped playing with the locket and started rearranging the papers on her desk. Her cheeks were a lovely shade of pink.

"Yes. We agree," Nan said.

"And...you're here to question me because I'm a mortician...a suspect?"

"Yes. Because you are a mortician and because you have the facilities to...shall we say...do the work."

"There are many morticians and many mortuaries in the area."

"Tell us about it," Nan laughed. "We've sorted through a few dozen. Done preliminary interviews with a few.

"You're married…to Peter Cromwell?" I asked.

"Yes."

"Has he had training as a mortician?" I continued.

"He's a CPA."

"That wasn't the question."

"I've given him some training. He assists me when we're very busy."

"Could he embalm a person without your assistance?"

"I suppose so. But he has no license, so I must be there whenever we're preparing someone…a loved one for presentation."

"What type of personal vehicle do you own?" Nan asked.

"My personal vehicle?"

"Yes."

"I drive a Volvo…2008…black sedan. It has a number of some sort, which escapes me now. It's out front. I can send Uncle Dan out to check if…" `

"Not necessary," I said. "We can do it on our way out. And what does Mr. Cromwell drive?"

"He has two cars...a Ford Focus he drives to work...and a Cadillac Escalade we use on trips...vacations and such."

"Have either of you ever attended classes at Hillsborough Community College?" Nan asked.

"Peter has attended some continuing education classes...at the main campus."

"Do you know the subject of those classes?"

"Data processing updates...for his business."

"You don't happen to know his instructor's name, do you?"

"No. Should I? Is it important?" Her responses were guarded, no longer Southern Comfort sweet.

"Could be," Nan said. "We need to ask if you'd be willing to sit for a polygraph examination?"

"Is it necessary?"

"Could go a long way in clearing your name."

"I understand they have no legal merit." Adrianna had now regressed to playing with her locket once more.

"No...not in court. But they do give direction for investigative purposes."

"I...don't know. I'd better talk to Peter about it. Would you expect him to do it, also?"

"Yes," I said.

"We'll call with a decision."

"Soon?"

"Yes."

"Good. One other question. Do you have a relationship with the Samuelson College of Mortuary Science?"

"Yes. I teach a class there. Two or three times a year." "Currently?" One last question led to another.

"Yes. One evening class."

"Were you there last night?"

"Yes."

"Last night, did you make a call using one of their phones?"

"I may have called home."

"May have?"

"I think I called Peter."

"Do you know Sheri Samuelson Parnell?"

"Yes. We're friends."

"Okay. That's about it...for now." I turned to Nan, "Do you have any other questions for Ms. Cromwell?"

"One."

"Yes?"

"Your lipstick. I adore that shade. Could you tell me what it is and where you buy it?"

19

I received a real shocker that night at the dinner table. Dad and Midge had been inordinately quiet since we'd said grace and started to eat. Dad broke the silence.

"I've sold the company."

"You've what?"

"Sold Paxton Construction to Easterling. Twenty million now…Annual payments based on a percentage of profits for twenty years."

"Easterling's one of your fiercest competitors, for God's sake."

"An honest man…does exceptional work."

"He's located thirty miles from here. What will your people do?"

"No problem. He's taking over the works. Our buildings, crews, equipment, office staff. Going to take my word on an operations manager here. He'll report directly to Easterling."

"I suppose you've got someone in mind?"

"I'd recommend you, but you enjoy playing detective too much."

"Playing detective?" I was upset before. Now I was damned mad and Midge knew it. She reached over and took my hand.

"Dad didn't mean it like it sounded," she said.

"Like hell I didn't," he said. "There's been a Paxton Construction on the same site for sixty-five years. Hate to see it end."

"Then why sell out? You didn't even ask me. Didn't even ask me what I thought."

"Knew what the answer would be. You haven't been interested in the company since you started wearing that shiny little badge."

I stared at him. This wasn't my father. Gruff. Insulting. I loved him too much not to cut him a little slack. "So…what will you do? Do you have any ideas? You're not built for sitting around."

"Travel for awhile until I get…over everything. Had Mary Jane book me on an forty-five day world cruise from Miami."

"Moving kind of fast, aren't you?"

"Never been slow about anything once I made up my mind. Proposed to your mother a month after we met."

He had changed and the reason was obvious. I suspected he'd never be the same. He carried his grief in his shirt pocket close to his heart.

He stood up. Looked at me and there was affection in his eyes. "I had this place deeded to you and Midge. I'll stay in the place next door when I get back."

The place next door was our former residence. The house he'd built for us. I looked at Midge. She smiled and licked a tear from her upper lip. I'd married a real softy.

* * *

Peter Cromwell was a good match for Adrianna, his gorgeous wife. He had strong, distinct features: high forehead; square, cleft chin; a generous mouth; and black wavy hair. All in all, a handsome dude akin to those lover boys in the era when cinema types were handsome dudes—among the most memorable, Robert Taylor, Gary Grant, Clark Gable, Errol Flynn, and Tyrone Power.

Cromwell's welcome was friendly and showed no signs of apprehension. "Hello. You are Detectives

Paxton and Delacorte? If I remember correctly, you carried the nickname of Rock when you were playing football."

"That was a long time ago. Ancient history," I said.

"Not that long ago...at least I don't like to think so. I played for Plant High when you were playing for Armwood. I got one shot to tackle you and missed to my everlasting shame. You were...probably still are...one tough dude."

"Overrated," I said. It was hard not to like the guy. I glanced at Nan. She appeared to be on the verge of a swoon—or a giggle. Her reaction to things was often mysteriously hers alone.

Cromwell put a chair at his desk for Nan. I grabbed one for myself.

"Now...where to start...oh yes, Adrianna said you requested we submit to a polygraph...relative to the Mortician murders."

"That's correct, as one means of ruling you folks out as suspects," I said.

"Personally, I have no objection. However, Adrianna is very concerned that nervousness could make it appear that she wasn't being truthful."

"You don't share her concern?" Nan asked. She'd gotten her tongue back.

"Not really," Cromwell flashed a Robert Taylor smile. Nan crossed her legs.

"Okay," I said, "I'll schedule an examination for you, and you can report back to your wife…tell her it didn't hurt a bit."

"Hold it, Detective. Although I don't share Adrianna's concern, I did check with the family attorney, and he recommended against it."

"For what reason?"

"Basically, because of the lack of reliability…our responses might be misinterpreted. Taken out of context. That sort of thing"

"Who is your attorney…if I may ask?"

"Perry…Preston Perry. You've heard of him?"

"I dated his daughter, April…in high school." A vision of April as she was flitted across my mind's eye—to coin a phrase that someone else had already coined.

"What a marvelous coincidence. I'll mention our meeting to him the next time I see him. By the way, she's on her way back to Tampa. She has a problem of sorts."

"What kind of problem?" I asked.

"A health problem of some sort. Something that wasn't handled too well in Britain…socialized medicine and all."

I stared at this amiable, outgoing man and suddenly realized something. He'd followed a script and taken me along. He knew about April and me. He knew about my football career and used it to flatter me. I suspected that he'd never played for Plant City. I'd check on it. It was time to get back to work.

"Adrianna said that you'd taken data processing classes at Hillsborough Community College. That correct?"

"Yes, many times."

"At the main campus on Dale Mabry?"

"Yes. Several classes there over the years."

"Ever take a course at the Ybor City campus?"

"Well…yes."

"Recently?"

"The last term. Fall term." The pace of my questioning seemed to bother him. He'd lost control of the situation and was showing signs of discomfort.

"Do you recall the instructor's name?"

"Why…yes…Selby. Georgia Selby."

"How well did you get to know Professor Selby?"

"We had a friendly relationship…I suppose I could say that."

"Okay, It was friendly. How friendly? Did she ever suggest that you and she get together after class for a drink or something?"

I sensed that he wanted to lie, but realized that was a black hole of sorts. "We did get together a few times."

"At her place?"

"Yes…at her place."

"Did your relationship develop into something more than a drink or two? Before you answer, I should tell you that we've had several very frank discussions with Professor Selby."

"Okay, we had a relationship."

"Sexual?"

"Yes, damn it."

"Had a relationship or you're having one?" I was on a roll, hitting the mark with every question.

"Yes…having…having…having. Where the hell is this going? I'm an adulterer. What's that to you, Detective Paxton?"

"Relax Mr. Cromwell. We're just about finished."

"I hope to God you are."

"Did you ever meet Ms. Selby's roomer, Billy Rock-efeller?"

"No. He was usually sacked out when I was there."

"You know he was murdered?"

"Of course."

"Where were you on the evening he was picked up by the person who killed him?" I gave him the date.

He leafed back through his desk calendar and frowned. "Can't say. Probably at home."

"That's not a very good alibi. Was your wife also at home? We'll check with her, you know."

"Check If you like. Now I'd appreciate it if you'd leave. Any future interviews will be attended by our lawyer, Preston Perry."

That should be interesting, I thought, as Nan and I left the office, lacking a handshake and an escort.

In our vehicle, Nan patted me on the back, smiled, and said, "Nice work, partner. You smoked him out… the handsome, cheating bastard."

"Thanks," I said. Modesty kept me for saying more.

"Wonder why a guy with a wife as lovely as Adrianna would screw around with a nympho number like Georgia?" Nan said.

"One for the money and two for the show."

"That fits," Nan said.

20

A week passed after our interview with pretty boy Cromwell, and we hadn't reached an agreement on the time and date for another interview with him and Adrianna. Lots of excuses passed back and forth: Preston Perry had a major case that demanded his full attention; Cromwell himself was caught up in a corporate tax matter that required several trips to Washington; and Adrianna was bogged down with bodies and burials.

Nan and I had interviewed Georgia Selby a third time and found her chilly and uncooperative. She copped to an ongoing affair with Peter Cromwell, calling him a "gutless bastard" after we told her that he'd admitted the affair.

So there we were. Much of what we had I found out during our investigation—now over three months old—brought us back to Georgia Selby and her affairs with Peter Cromwell and Victor Parnell. Nan and I sat down with the Lieutenant to discuss the possibilities as we saw them.

* * *

"And where is all of this leading?" Luis asked after we attempted to explain our lack of progress. "I Take it you're not even close to wrapping it up. I've got to tell you that the Mayor is interested because of the embalmed pup that got deposited on her stoop. Since she's interested, Major Tankersly is interested. And when the Major is interested, I get interested…very interested." Major Beryl Tankersly was the head of the Major Crimes Division, which included homicide.

"We have two very plausible scenarios, Luis. First… and the most straight forward…we could accept the reasonable possibility that there are a couple of nuts out there who believe they're carrying out a mission of mercy. One or both is a professional mortician with access to a mortuary. We have three couples who fit the bill…none of whom has a history of anti-social…criminal behavior. No rap sheets."

"Okay. Who are these duos?"

"Adrianna Cromwell...owner of the Loving Shepherd Mortuary and Cemetery and husband Peter, who's a CPA. Then, there's Victor Parnell...operates the Parnell family's crematorium...and his wife Sheri Samuelson Parnell who teaches at the Samuleson College of Mortuary Science."

"Okay. That's two?" It was a question.

"There's a Samuelson son...Dustan Junior and wife Nina. He and his wife travel the country procuring cadavers for the college. We felt they appeared a trifle nervous the only time we caught them in town. We understand they're in and out a lot. Very hard to pin down"

"They're not really on your list of favorites?"

"Not off as yet. Marginal," Nan said. "And the scenario Rock described isn't our favorite scenario, either."

Luis looked at Nan, then at me. "Shoot...one of you."

I nodded to Nan and she took over. "We think the murder of Mary O'Malley was committed solely as a ploy to mislead us."

"Mislead you. How?"

"By making us believe the subsequent murder of William Rockefeller was also done by a pair of screwballs on a crusade. We see it as an attempt to steer us away from the real motive."

"Which was?"

"William Rockefeller's millions," I stepped in. "Georgia Selby ...Rockefeller's landlady...has had affairs with Victor Parnell and Peter Cromwell. She has a copy of Rockefeller's will and has known for some time what she'd inherit when Billy died. Nan and I believe she may have colluded with one or both of her pretty boy lovers to set up the whole charade...the dog embalming...the O'Malley murder."

"Sounds good, but do you have any solid proof? Sounds like a damned good theory, but theories don't lead to convictions...as you both know."

"Sure we know, Lieutenant," I said. "We're looking at five very bright people...maybe seven...all of whom except Selby refuse a polygraph. We have no idea which of the two men Selby brought in on the deal. Maybe she tried Victor Parnell and he refused, so she went to Peter Cromwell. We don't know if either of the wives know...we believe one does...the one who picked up Mary O'Malley...and she could have been a hire."

"Okay...where are you going from here?" Luis asked

"We'd like to plant someone in one of Selby's up-coming classes. Next term starts in ten days. Have to be a bright, good looking, engaging guy who could stimulate her predatory interest in younger men...if that's what it is. We'll find out fast if she's always on the hunt or whether she hunted until she got the guy she wanted for a specific purpose. Murder."

"Young, handsome, and engaging? Could he be Hispanic?"

"Why not...she might find a Latin lover enticing."

"I have a nephew who's a tech in Systems Main-tenance and helps out in Internet Crimes. My sister's boy...they say he looks like me."

"Is he as old as you?" Nan asked.

"Twenty-nine...maybe thirty. Hey...I'll call and get him up here. See if he's interested in being used as bait to catch a hot momma.

"Is he married?" I asked

"No. He's very intelligent."

* * *

Ten minutes after Luis' call, his nephew arrived. He was tall, with dark eyes, wavy black hair, and a wide smile. He flashed the smile at Nan, and I watched as she arched her back and crossed her legs. By displaying two of her better features, I surmised that she approved the nephew for some undercover work.

"This is my nephew, Hernando Wright," Luis said with pride spilling over his lean features.

"Wright?" Nan thought she'd misunderstood Luis.

"Yes...my sister...his mother married an Anglo. Other than that, she's a good person."

We all laughed. Nan almost had hysterics. Then Luis explained our proposition to Hernando. After which, he asked, "Sounds like fun. When do I start?"

Part Three

Any protracted activity involving more than two individuals may lead to unanticipated outcomes for innocent participants when one of the number has a
hidden and perverse agenda.

CBW - 08

21

It was near bedtime. Midge and I were cuddling on the library veranda when we heard someone enter the house. I jumped up and my right hand went toward my left side where I carried my weapon. I recalled that it was in our bedroom at the other end of the house. I started toward the sound, picking up a bronze statue as I went. The tension was suddenly eased when Dad's voice shattered the peaceful night. The tree frogs and the crickets stopped chirping and listened.

"Where are you guys? Rock...it's Dad. Where the hell are you?"

"Library," I shouted back. Midge straightened up her nightgown, and I buttoned my shirt. We managed to turn on table and floor lamps before Dad reached us. He wasn't alone.

After hugging us, he turned to his companion. "This, kids, is Denise Roberts Paxton...my wife and...I guess, your step mom, son."

"My...step mom? You two are married? This is...a surprise."

"A welcome one, I hope." Denise Roberts Paxton extended a long fingered hand, which I took with some hesitation. Maybe I was afraid I might like her. Her hand was warm. Her handshake, firm. "I won't hurt you Brad...Rock. To the contrary, I'm almost afraid of you. Based on all the things your father has told me, I thought I'd be meeting Superman." She had a warm throaty voice. Her laugh was genuine. There was something else about her that bothered me.

Dad saw it in my eyes.

"Looks like Mom, doesn't she?"

She did. She was slightly taller than Mom had been. But her appearance otherwise was as I remembered mother when I was in high school. Her brown eyes danced a little when she smiled. Not overweight, but slightly thick in the waist. Mom's aprons would fit her well.

"Met Denise on the cruise ship. She's a widow...like me... well...I mean, we've both lost our spouses recently."

"I really wasn't looking for a husband," Denise said, putting her arm around Dad's waist and looking up into his face. "But your father's extremely persuasive. A good salesman…a handsome one."

I looked at Dad and had to agree. I'd never thought of him as handsome, but he was, particularly with the deep tan he'd acquired on his forty-five day cruise around the world.

"You guys appear to be ready for bed," Dad said, "and Denise and I are pooped…so would you help us with our luggage, Rock. We parked at the other place. Oh…I've got to warn you…Denise and her late husband were missionaries, so don't use any dirty words in her presence."

"Don…darn you…you'll make them think I'm some sort of prude. I've seen and worked with and around more evil…more vulgarity than you'll ever see or hear in this neck of the woods."

"So you say," he said, laughed, and put his powerful hands under her arms and lifted her above his head as though she were a small child.

"I'll get your bags," I said, "if you put the nice lady down and give me some help." It was Saturday evening, which was great. I knew I would sleep much better that night. I hadn't told Midge, but I'd been worried about him, afraid I'd never see him again.

* * *

"Yes. You heard me right. Dad came back from his cruise with a brand new wife."

"Mistake?" Nan asked from where she was perched on the corner of my desk.

"I don't think so. She's no phony...and you won't believe this...except for an inch or so in height...mom could have been her twin. He's nuts about her...I believe the resemblance to Mom has a lot to do with it. Anyway, he sure as hell loves her, and she apparently reciprocates in spades. Treats him just as Mom did. Tones him down. Brings out the gentleness in him. Spent all day yesterday with them. He's happy again. And I'm damned glad for him...and for her."

"I'll send them a card," Nan said.

"Better send it soon. They're already scheduling a trip to Venice and beyond."

"I'll give them a call."

"Better wait. They're probably still in bed."

"Tired from their trip?"

"I think there's more to it than fatigue."

"You're kidding. How old is Don?"

"A very young fifty two."

"Does virility run the family?"

"Absolutely," I said with a growl while offering my biceps for her to touch. She abstained.

* * *

Through the kitchen window, Marian watched the lights of Mort's vehicle strike the barn door and watched the door open and close after the vehicle entered. For a nostalgic moment, she recalled how much she had once looked forward to his return to the farm or to the Tampa condo.

Now, fear throttled her as she waited. She knew who he was now--an egomaniac, a manipulator, and a sadist. She also knew that she couldn't escape him. He'd warned her in explicit terms that any effort on her part to placate her conscience by going to the police would be fatal to members of her family and, ultimately, to her.Additionally, with the objective of in-suring her silence, he began following her and show-ing up unexpectedly at any time--morning, evening, and any hour between. On each such occasion, he'd pretend the meeting was a mere coincidence. Then--to demonstrate that it wasn't--he'd grip her arm and tell her how concerned he was about her health. Tell her that she shouldn't spend so much time away from her work. That it could lead to temptations she couldn't resist.

He'd also installed recorders on all of their phones and had disposed of several cell phones, saying that he'd read that their use could cause brain tumors. And that he'd never forgive himself if she became ill.

* * *

Mort wasn't alone when he emerged from the darkness into the light over the back stoop. His right arm was around the waist of an old woman with unkempt white hair and bleary eyes. She stumbled. Mort said something to her, and her cackling response drove Marian to her bedroom where she locked the door and fell upon the bed, sobbing, "No…no not again. Not another one."

A knock on the bedroom door pulled her upright. "Dear. I know you're up. I saw you in the window. We have a lovely guest, and I promised her one of your fabulous home-cooked dinners. I know you won't disappoint her…or me."

22

Hernando Wright paid rapt attention to Professor Georgia Selby as she introduced herself to the class in Document Formatting with Microsoft Office.

As she introduced herself, her bright, inquisitive eyes briefly touched those of each member of the class of fifteen students—nine women and six men. She completed her opening remarks by reading the course description from the catalog.

"Are there any questions?" she asked and waited. "Are we all certain we're in the right course. I know I am, how about you all?"

Following the laugh that followed, she asked the students to give their names and tell "a little something" about themselves. Because his surname began with a W, Hernando was the last to be called, there being no Xaviers, Yoders, or Zambranos in the class.

"Mr. Hernando Wright…you're up. Last, but certainly not least." Georgia eyes measured him for a suit. A swim suit.

Hernando stood and faced his classmates. Tall, straight, dark and at complete ease, he said, "People wonder about my Anglo last name…it's English, you know. There's a simple explanation. My father was the only Anglo left in South Miami. My mother needed an interpreter to communicate with someone in Tampa, so she took him on…in a literal sense. I was the result of a misinterpretation."

After the laughter ended, Georgia asked, "And what do you do for a living beside telling little white lies, Mr. English Latino?"

"Seriously?" he turned to face Georgia.

"Seriously," she said.

"I work in the call center for Brinks Home Security."

"I'm surprised. I think most of the ladies here would see you in a more glamorous situation." Some tittering and nodding followed.

"I was told if I took some courses like this, I could expect a promotion to something more…not glamorous…more profitable."

"You're to be congratulated for being such a practical young man. Thanks for the fun Mr. Wright." The class—at least the women—applauded as Hernando flashed his wide, white, and engaging smile.

* * *

By arrangement, Nan and I met with Hernando the morning after his introduction to Georgia Selby.

"How did it go?" I asked.

"Okay, I believe," he said and then described the repartee associated with his introduction. "If progress means she made some moves…she didn't. If it means she seemed interested, she did. Interested but cautious, I'd say."

"Sounds promising," Nan said.

"I think so. I waited until the rest of the class left the room and approached her. Told her I wanted to apologize for my attempt to be funny."

"What was her reaction?"

"Said it was okay. The fun. That every class needs some comic relief. Asked her if I should wear a Donald Duck mask for the next class. She frowned and said she preferred the one I had one. Asked where I bought it."

"You were correct about her being cautious," I said. "The Brinks operator got a call this morning…woman caller who asked for you. The operator handled it as we agreed. Told her you'd be in at 10 a.m."

"And if she calls at 10 a. m.?" Hernando asked.

"Call will be transferred to you on my line," I said.

"You think she will…call again?"

"I doubt it. If her libido is cooking…which it probably is…she'll only be a trifle cautious."

"Damn. How very exhilarating," Hernando said and grinned to sharpen the point on his point.

* * *

We'd just returned from lunch when the Lieutenant called us in. "Owner of the Meeting Place bar in North Tampa opened for the day and found a customer who didn't need a libation. She was dead and all prettied up like an undertaker had worked on her. Looks like one of yours. Here's the address." Luis handed me the address on a page torn from a spiral note pad and said goodbye.

At the Meeting Place, we found a white-haired lady in a delightfully frilly J.C. Penney creation occupying one of eight booths along one wall in the barroom side of the small eatery. She was—as suspected—prepped for burial. Mort and Marian had found another victim.

The note pinned to her dress was brief, and the message was consistent with prior communications:

Mayor and Commissioners:

Did you think I was gone? No way. I'll be leaving my little messages around town until you political types do more to help our destitute street people. By the way, I didn't believe for a minute your planted stories about Mary and Billy being well off. You're not dealing with an idiot, as I think your detectives already know. The Mortician

Nan and I sat down with the owner of The Meeting Place after the crime scene techs had done their thing and the body had been removed by the coroner's wagon after they confirmed what we already knew. The lady had been embalmed.

The bar owner's name was Jim Askew. We learned that he knew the little, white-haired lady in the new dress. She was a neighborhood boozer who hung around outside his place until someone offered to buy her a drink.

"At first, I thought she'd be bad for business, but some regulars took a shine to her—called her Wino Winnie. Asked about her when she wasn't around," he said.

"Wino Winnie? Was her name Winnie? Winifred?" Nan asked.

"As I said, she called herself Winnie. Customers added the 'Wino'. She did say her full name was Winnie Mae Houser."

Askew's reference to "his regulars" reminded me that Nan and I now carried a photo display of our suspects and a few ringers, which had been put together by our techs from a collection of snapshots and newspaper articles. Included in the line up were Adrianna and Peter Cromwell; Victor and Sheri Parnell; Dustan Samuelson, Jr. and wife, Nina; and, last but not least, Georgia Selby.

"Would you mind looking at a some photos and see if you recognize anyone," I asked the cooperative bar owner.

"Anything to help, Detective."

"Nan, would you mind?"

"I'm on the way, partner," she said. And, having anticipated my request, she was already at the door headed for our vehicle to retrieve the photo display.

Two minutes later, Jim Askew was scrutinizing the photo collection.

It was several minutes before he made a decision. "Yeah… these two…they used to come here a lot. Two or three times a week." His index fingers were resting on two very bad photos of Peter Cromwell and Georgia Selby.

"Are you certain?" Nan asked.

"Yeah…pictures aren't too good…but the guy's Pete and the woman is Georgie. Pete calls her Georgie Girl."

"You know their last names?"

"Nope. All I ever heard was Pete and Georgie. They were close…sometimes too hot and heavy for my taste…you know, like getting it on in public. They haven't been in for a few weeks, which don't make me feel bad."

23

At the end of the third class session, Georgia Selby invited Hernando to stay behind to discuss his work.

When the classroom was empty, he asked, "Have I done something out of line, Ms. Selby?"

"Heavens no. It's just that you seem to know a lot more about the subject matter than most of the others in the class. Perhaps you should be in another class…a more advanced class."

"I read a lot of technical stuff…probably more than most. I truly believe that your class is helping fill in some gaps for me."

"I certainly hope so. I wouldn't want you to waste your time or money."

"If I thought that, I wouldn't stay in the class…and that's a promise."

"You aren't married, are you, Hernando?"

"No. Not even a little bit."

"That's hard to believe. You're such a very handsome young man."

"Thanks, Ms. Selby. To be honest, I enjoy the freedom of a bachelor life...if you know what I mean."

"I certainly do know what you mean. You know that I'm not married either, don't you?" she said as she began putting her materials from her desk into a black leather briefcase.

"That's hard to believe...you being such an attractive woman," he said, glancing at her breasts. She smiled in acceptance of the double barreled tribute.

"Do you drink, Hernando?" She walked toward the door. He followed.

"Everything but tequila. I swore off tequila when I learned that it was created by Mexican peasants who put worms in it to keep the upper class from stealing it."

"Good Lord, I never heard that."

"Neither did I. I just made it up as a reasonable repudiation. Truth is, I just don't like the damned stuff."

"You get a kick out of teasing, don't you?" She flipped off the classroom lights and turned to face him.

"If it's justified by the situation."

"Would you be embarrassed if you were seen with me in public?"

"Embarrassed? Why would I be?"

"I'm somewhat older than you."

"So…good wine is normally somewhat older than bad wine."

"Well…we'll see. Good night, Hernando. We'll talk again next Wednesday night…maybe we'll do a little wine tasting after."

"That a promise?" he asked.

"We'll see," she said.

* * *

Nan and I finally got a second interview with Peter Cromwell. Still tied up with a major case, Preston Perry sent daughter April to represent the firm. April had been my senior prom sweetheart at Armwood High. To say that I was shocked by her appearance—as understatements go—was equivalent to saying hydrogen bombs could be slightly destructive.

She spoke first. "Hello, Rock. You're looking well," she said and took my hand, reaching across the table in the in the interview room.

"Thanks, April. I heard you were back in Tampa." I wanted to tell her that she looked well, too, but she didn't. She was thin. Emaciated. Her clothes hung limply on a slender frame that had once carried enough flesh to make her one of the most physically attractive women I'd ever known.

Nan and I sat at the table across from April and Cromwell. They waited for me to speak, so I did.

"We will be taping this interview for future reference…if you and your Counsel have no objection, Mr. Cromwell."

"I have no objection, detective," Cromwell said after getting the nod from April,

"For the record…you denied our previous request for you to submit to a polygraph examination. Is that correct?"

"Yes…that's correct."

"Are you now willing to submit to an examination?"

"No, I am not."

"Please explain your reason for not agreeing to same."

"It has been shown that such examinations lack reliability in determining the truthfulness of an examinee's responses."

"And what can you cite as the basis for that conclusion?" I asked, knowing that all of his answers would have been prepared and approved by April.

"If it were a valid investigative tool, the conclusions of such examinations could and would be submitted as evidence in a court of law. They can't be." Cromwell smirked and glanced at April for approval. I nodded and moved on.

"There was another murder last week by the person who calls himself the Mortician," I said. "Have you heard about it?"

"Yes."

"How did you learn of it?"

"I don't recall. Someone mentioned it...in passing."

"Could that someone have been Jim Askew?"

"Jim Askew? I don't recognize the name."

"How about Wino Winnie? Ever heard that name before?"

"Oh...Winnie...yes. Old woman that hangs out at that bar on North Dale Mabry, The Meeting Place. And, yeah...now I recall...the bar owner's name is Askew. I'd completely forgotten it. Haven't been there for several weeks."

"Come on, Peter. You didn't forget. You were evading the question. Why? Anything to do with Georgie Girl?"

Cromwell's jaw hardened. He turned and whispered something into April's ear. She looked at me and said, "I need a few minutes alone with my client, detectives. Would you mind?"

* * *

We watched on the closed circuit TV as Peter and April carried on an animated conversation in the interview room.

"Looks as though dear Peter held out on his counselor," Nan said.

"Does appear that way. She has him wiggling in his chair, the arrogant s.o.b."

"What do you think, partner? You believe that he's our guy? Like…are you any more certain than you were before we made the connection with Georgie Girl?" Nan asked.

"Can't really say that I am. The main campus of the Community College is only a few miles south of The Meeting Place, and he admitted that the affair with Selby started after he took a class she taught."

"But…what about Wino Winnie? Just a coincidence that she ends up dead in a bar that two of our suspects frequented?"

"That does add some weight to our case against… hey…here we go. The counselor's calling us back."

I stood to leave and Nan grabbed my arm. "You turned white when you saw her, Rock. She must have meant a lot to you. Remember this, I'm with you friend…you need to talk, I'm here for you any damned time and any damned place." I looked into her face and saw something I never thought I'd see in her eyes. Tears. Tears for me.

"Thanks, Nan," I said, choking a little. "We'd better get in there before she kills him.

* * *

Back in our chairs facing a stern-faced April Perry and her chastened client, I said, "You guys straight now?"

"Yes…we've reached an understanding. My client unwisely withheld information about his liaison with Ms. Georgia Selby… something he'd previously con-fessed to you…something I should have known. He's put me in a difficult situation, a situation that requires a thorough clarification before we can continue our attorney-client relationship."

"That mean you're calling the interview over...for now?"

"That it does," April said.

"Will it be possible to continue next week, Counselor?" Nan asked.

"I'll call," she said. She looked at Cromwell and added, "Peter would you go on without me? I need to talk to Detective Paxton."

"I'll show Mr. Cromwell out," Nan said. Then April and I were alone.

* * *

"It's so good to see you, Rock. Hug me please."

I pulled her close and kissed her cheek. "God... what's happened to you, April?"

"I'm skinny, huh?" She laughed like it didn't matter, but I knew it did. "Believe it or not, I've gained eight pounds since I got home. I picked up malaria on a trip to the Sudan for the firm. Doc's say I'll be as good as new in another six or seven weeks."

"That's great news, kid."

"I think so. How's Midge?"

"Pregnant...but on the move."

"Pregnant. She's a lucky woman," April said.

"She thinks so," I said. "Damn, it's good to see you April. Good memories die hard."

"Perhaps we can talk over old times…over lunch someday."

"That would be great. I'll bring Midge along."

"How did I know you'd say that?" she said as she turned and walked away. As always, she left with a piece of my heart.

24

It was Tuesday night. They sat facing each other in a booth in the darkest corner of a back alley Ybor city bar. Georgia Selby reached across the table and touched her incensed companion's hand.

"What the hell do you mean...break it off, Georgia? I haven't heard a reason that makes any damned sense. None at all."

"It's just what I said. The police are looking at me as a murder suspect. And...believe me...I've done absolutely nothing to warrant suspicion. Absolutely nothing. Perhaps I've been a little indiscreet in my choice of companions...but absolutely nothing beyond that."

"And I'm one of your indiscretions? I'll tell you something straight out, Georgia, when I say it's quits, that's when it's over. Not one second before. Do you under-stand me? Am I clear?"

"Being unreasonable won't change things, Dustan. I won't be accused of a murder just because a com-panion happens to be a mortician. I shouldn't think you'd want to become a suspect because of your pro-fession and your association with me."

Staring at her, his mind raced. He recognized his vulnerability. But he cared for her...no matter what kind of bitch she was.

"Okay Georgia, I won't bother you any more...for now. But I'll leave you with something to consider. I know things about you... things you believe are se-crets. I'll be quiet for awhile...but someday I could change my mind. And one other thing...if I find you're dumping me for another guy...there'll be a price to pay. For both of you."

He rose from the booth and left Georgia unshak-en...left her considering her options. She had several, but she'd have to choose wisely.

* * *

Hernando found Georgia Selby particularly cool when he entered her Wednesday night class. He smiled at her and she nodded but didn't return the smile. He shrugged and went to the computer station he'd selected on the first night of class. "Life goes go on," he muttered. "Maybe it's that time of the month."

When the class ended, he waited for the room to empty before approaching her. She was at her desk and didn't look up, but did recognize his presence.

"Sorry I misled you, Hernando. You and I wouldn't be a good thing. I think it best that we aren't seen together outside of the classroom."

"What's changed, Georgia? I was looking forward to us having a drink or two after class, and maybe something else after."

"So was I, Hernando."

"So what's the explanation for the change of heart?"

"To be totally honest, there's a man I dated a few times…he won't leave me alone. He threatened me… said if he ever saw me with another man, there'd be trouble for me and my companion. I wouldn't want you endangered by being seen with me."

"Hell…I'm a big boy. I can handle myself okay…especially against cowardly types who get their kicks by bullying women."

"I appreciate your…bravery…but I'm not talking fisticuffs, dear. I believe the man I'm talking about would…kill to keep me. I realize that may sound hyperbolic, but he has this fixation…it defies rationality. I've never, never encouraged him. Honestly."

"So…why don't you report him? Call a cop?"

"Go to the police? He's a very prominent man, Hernando, and all I have is my word that he threatened me…or threatened the man I choose over him."

"So…where does that leave us? You and me?"

As a response to his question, she stood and walked around her desk. She leaned against him and touched his lips with her finger tips.

"Well…if you're really that eager to take a chance just to be with me…I could leave by myself, drive home and freshen up…and wait for you at my place."

"Two questions. How do I get there? And how long does it take you to freshen up?"

* * *

He watched Georgia's car leave the College parking lot. When her vehicle was out of sight, he followed and drove directly to a parking spot where he could see her leave her garage and enter the rear door of the house. When her bedroom light came on and the vertical blinds closed, he left his vehicle and went to her front door and quietly inserted the key she'd given him several weeks earlier. He wondered if she'd for-gotten about the key? Did she expect him to come to her...despite saying she thought it best for them to break up? Perhaps she wanted to spice up their re-lationship. To titillate him. She had. He was breathing rapidly when he entered her bedroom.

She was in the shower. He crossed the bedroom and entered the bathroom. Opening the shower door, he smiled, and said, "Surprise. You were expecting me, weren't you, you ornery little devil?" He removed his jacket and began unbuttoning his shirt. "We'll shower together."

She stepped from the shower and pushed him aside. "What in the hell are you doing here?" she said, while wrapping herself in a towel taken from a hook on the back of the bathroom door. "I told you it was over. Now, button up and get the hell out of my house...my life."

He followed her into the bedroom. "Damn you, you bitch. I know you saw me in the parking lot. You knew I'd follow you."

"How would I know you'd be that stupid? Oh...and give me that key I gave to you...like an idiot. Do it...if you don't..."

It was then that she heard footsteps on the staircase. A smile touched her lips. Throwing the towel on the floor, she threw herself on the bed and screamed, "Don't...please don't hurt me."

25

Hernando Wright's eyes flashed with anger at the sight of Georgia naked on her bed and a bewildered man with an unbuttoned shirt standing over her. He didn't hesitate. In four long strides, he reached what he perceived to be an attacker. His shoulder hit the culprit in the chest and drove him to the floor. Kneeling astride the downed man, he threw three quick punches that broke through the defensive arc formed by the downed man's arms and ended his resistance.

"For God's sake, get off of me. Are you crazy? Who the hell are you?" Blood from a split lip ran down the man's chin.

Hernando stood slowly, his hands still curled in hard knots. "Is this the s. o. b. you told me about, Georgia?"

"Yes...it is. My towel please, Hernando." When the towel was returned, she covered herself and got out of the bed. Looking at the bewildered man kneeling on the floor, she said, "This pathetic cretin is

Dustan Samuelson."

"The guy who owns that College of Mortuary... whatever?"

"No. This is Junior. He's a ghoul...a body collector for his father."

Seeing that his attacker was engaged holding the "frightened" Georgia Selby, Samuelson stood and said, "You mind if I go to the bathroom and clean my face, hero?"

Hernando's face reddened. "Do what you're got to do, punk. Then get the hell out of here."

"Not before he returns my key," Georgia said, clinging to her newly found Galahad.

* * *

Lieutenant Luis Agosto paced while three of us watched, waiting for the flames to subside. Hernando sat between Nan and me. Hernando's description of the confrontation with Dustan Samuelson had prompted Luis' display of vexation. None of us quite certain what was coming. Ridicule. Outrage. A simple critique.

Luis stopped pacing and dropped into the plush desk chair that had once belonged to his beloved predecessor, Captain Dewayne Jackson. "I think you were tricked Hernando, by a very smart woman...a very smart woman who seems to collect men who make their livings off of corpses. Since you are not one who does that, I think she may actually like you...since you are my nephew and, naturally, a very handsome man. All of this leaves us with a question. Why did she choose to have affairs with three men...all with some training as morticians? Or did they seek her out for some illegal enterprise?"

After a short silence, I said, "Either a coincidence or an effort To complicate the investigation. I'd go with the latter, which would mean that Georgia read about Mary's murder, and went on the hunt for someone to help her with Billy Rockefeller. A copy cat murder with a financial motive."

"So, if the first murder gave her the idea to do away with Billy, we must accept the fact that there are two murderers with different motives...or two sets of murderers. Male and female pair ups...sort of mom and pop enterprises," Luis said. "Let's review the facts as we currently see them.. You start, Rock."

"Okay. We know for certain that one or both of the parties in all three murders has training in mortuary science. That applies to Dustan Samuelson and Victor Parnell. Peter Cromwell has been trained by his wife, Adrianna. Of the wives, both Sheri Samuelson and Adrianna are pros." I paused and Nan stepped in.

"Everything points to a man and woman in the Mary O'Malley murder and embalming. It's apparent that the kooky duo that did the dogs also did Mary. Our techs have confirmed there are definite similarities in the note materials left at the scene and also the materials used in the embalming process." She finished and glanced at me.

"Because of the pending inheritance and Georgia's penchant for mortician types, we've got to go with Georgia and one of the three male suspects. I'd rule Victor Parnell out. His relationship with Selby was very short lived…probably indicating she couldn't hook him. Selby dumped Dustan Samuelson…aided by Hernando. She'd hardly dump the person she planned to share her fortune with. In addition, Dustan is impulsive. Not as bright as the others. Not the type one would trust in a complex plot. So…that brings it to Peter Cromwell. A long run with Georgia and they frequented a bar where our third victim hung out...so to speak."

"There's a third possibility," Nan broke in, "perhaps Georgia had nothing to do with any of the murders, and it was...as we originally believed...the work of two nuts...a man and a woman who think they're relieving destitute people of the burden of living."

"There's also the possibility that one or more of the male suspects and their wives arranged or participated in the murders without Georgia's knowledge...after she told them of the fortune she would inherit. Figuring because of their relationship with her, they'd ditch their wives and cash in big time after probate."

"From what you told us, Hernando, you haven't been alone with her long enough to learn anything significant. Is that correct?"

"Yes, Lieutenant."

"Do you believe that you can gain her trust if you continue this undercover assignment?"

Hernando blushed. "I do believe she trusts me...I don't know whether she trusts me enough to confide in me about anything incriminating. Or whether she ever will trust me that much. And, as Detective Delacorte said, perhaps she has nothing to confess."

"So...to pin it down...do you believe there's anything to gain by your continued involvement with Ms. Selby?" Luis asked,

"I can't be certain...but perhaps."

"What do you think?" Luis looked at Nan and me.

"It can't hurt," Nan said.

"I agree," I said.

"A question, Hernando?" Luis said.

"Yes?"

"Do you think either you or Georgia have anything to fear from Samuelson?"

"I think he's a pussy cat," Hernando said in a burst of bravado.

"A suggestion," I said, looking at Hernando.

"What?"

"Watch your back, man. Some little feline types grow up to be very large and ferocious animals."

* * *

Sitting at a desk in the College's morgue suite, Dustan Samuelson relived his embarrassment at the hands of Georgia and her Latin friend. While holding an ice pack to his swollen jaw, thoughts of revenge occupied his mind, and--as he considered his options--he couldn't bring himself to believe that Georgia had used him. That she had no feelings for him. Never had. The bitch. The pig. And the Latin lover boy--she'd called him Hernando—had taken him by surprise. Knocked him to the floor. Humiliated him. No price could be too great for doing that.

"Hey, what happened to you, my man? Nina beat you up for sassin' her?" A voice interrupted his ruminations.

Dustan stared into the grinning face of the morgue attendant, Parker Turner, his brother-in-law.

"Hell, you know your Nina's no match for me, Parker."

"She sure as hell could handle me when we were kids," Parker said. "Seriously, what happened?"

"I came in late last night to pick up my travel schedule for the rest of the week. The floor was wet...guess it had just been mopped...and I slipped and banged my face on that damned packing case over there."

"Hey, I'll move it, Dustan."

"No problem, Parker. The damage is done. Wasn't your fault that I didn't take my schedule with me when I left yesterday."

"Can I do anything for you, bro?"

"Well…I'm going home to nurse my wounds. You could lie for me if anyone asks where I am. Tell them I had to make a call in Ocala."

"Can do, bro. Take it easy."

"That's the only way to take it, bro. Slow and easy."

26

Approximately ten days after our first interview with Peter Cromwell, April Perry called to set up a second interview. Nan had gone to the Loving Shepherd Cemetery for another go-round with Adrianna Cromwell. So I met with April and her "I'm beautiful, look me over" client.

They agreed to recording the interview, and I handed April a transcript of the first interview for reference and we took off.

"Mr. Cromwell, during your admitted relationship with Georgia Selby, did you discuss the inheritance she would receive in the event of William Rockefeller's death?"

"She may have mentioned it in passing. I wouldn't say we discussed it."

"In passing? You didn't have enough interest to ask how much it might be?"

"Well, yes, I suppose I might have asked."

"You suppose?"

"Yeah...suppose. How the hell am I expected to recall a conversation that occurred weeks ago." He almost growled. April intervened.

"I think he's answered as best he can, Detective Paxton. Can we move on?"

"Two more related questions, Counselor. Okay?"

"Depends on what they are. Don't expect Mr. Cromwell to incriminate himself."

"This conversation did occur before Rockefeller's murder?"

"That follows, doesn't it? Yes. The conversation did occur before the man's death."

"During the balance of your rather lengthy relationship with Ms, Shelby, was Mr. Rockefeller the subject of any further discussions?"

"Of course, when his body was discovered in the riverfront park. Georgia was very broken up over the murder. She liked him very much. I consoled her."

"Broken up? Strange. When my partner and I told her of the incident, she didn't seem that upset."

"So. Maybe she didn't want to get emotional in front of a couple of…cops."

"Maybe. How did you know Rockefeller's body was found in a riverfront park?"

"Saw it in the Tribune, I guess."

"It wasn't reported in the papers."

"Damned if I can remember how I found out…stuff like that gets around. People talk."

"Could you have heard it from a friend?"

"Always a possibility."

"A friend like Victor Parnell? Or Dustan Samuelson?"

"Who said they were my friends?"

"We were told that you folks got together…as couples."

"Yeah…for dinner a few times. The wives are friends. I'm not a friend of either of those…men."

* * *

I concluded the interview by confirming some of his responses at the first and second interviews. Once again, Cromwell left and April stayed behind for a hug. She looked some better and I told her so. She asked about Midge, the baby in the works, and I got her phone number. I promised to have Midge call.

I should mention my parting shot at Mister Lovely: "That's about it, Mr. Cromwell. By the way, I checked on your football career at Plant. You don't need to be ashamed of missing that tackle on me. It's hard to get a good bead on a guy from a seat in the bandstand."

27

Nan and I followed up our meetings with the Cromwell's by interviewing Dustan Samuelson, Jr., and his wife Nina. It was a week after his brush with Hernando. We'd delayed the sit down so that it wouldn't appear that there was a connection between TPD and the Latin tornado that had swept him off his feet on the prior Wednesday.

Dustan was a dark man. Approximately the same height as our other male suspects, he had black hair clipped short, heavy black eyebrows, dark eyes, and the type of beard that turns blue after a close shave. One side of his swarthy face still bore signs of Hernando's attack.

Nina was a slender Latino, five-five with a proud posture and a smile that was wide and complete with full lips and very perfect teeth.

After telling both that the interviews would be recorded, I took Dustan into one interview room while Nan took Nina into an adjacent cubicle. When we'd introduced ourselves to Dustan and Nina, I found myself comparing Dustan's appearance to that of his sister, Sheri Samuelson Parnell. The difference was significant. I asked him about it.

"I've met your sister Sheri…as you probably know… and there's such a difference in appearance between you two. There must be an explanation. Do you mind satisfying my curiosity?"

"Not at all. I'm the product of Dad's first little fling… legal but irrelevant. Sheri's the celebrated result of Dad's second glorious marriage. My mother died giving me life. I never knew her so you needn't say you're sorry to hear it." It was apparent that Dustan had told the story many times. It was also apparent that he didn't think much of his stepmother and half sister.

"You have bad feelings about Sheri and your stepmother?"

"No feelings whatsoever. They do their thing, and I do mine. As long as I get my rightful portion of Senior's money when he passes, I don't give a damn about them and what they do."

"You sound very bitter. And alienated."

"Must be because I am...look...I thought you brought us in to discuss those murders by a guy who calls himself the Mortician. I didn't expect you to shimmy up my family tree."

"Sorry. But it's all about learning something about a suspect's personality. Attitudes. Motivations. I'm certain that you're aware of the fact that family relationships have a lot to do with what we become, and what we're capable of doing or becoming."

"That's right. I am a suspect, and now that you know I don't give a diddley squat about any of them, I move up on the suspect list. Right? Maybe to the top. First time I've ever made the top of anyone's list."

"Do you believe you're capable of murder? Maybe taking out a couple of nobodies who no one will miss?"

"To be totally honest...if I wanted to take out anyone...Dad, step mom, and dainty little Sheri would be at the tip top of my hit list."

"You couldn't take out a couple of decrepit innocents as proxies for the people you really want to kill?"

"That what you believe?"

"I think you're a very angry man. Angry men can do anything under certain circumstances. Yes. I think you're capable of killing."

"Okay…that's out. Where do we go from there?"

"Two of our suspects have had sexual relationships with a community college instructor name of Georgia Selby. Do you know Ms. Selby?"

Samuelson glared at me. He was wondering what we knew and decided to take a chance. "The name isn't familiar."

"It's important for you to be honest, Mr. Samuelson. We have reason to believe you do know Ms. Selby…very well."

"Okay, Detective. You be honest with me. Has someone told you that I know her?"

"The question is yours to answer. I'll ask it again, if you like."

"Okay, damn you. I know Georgia. I, had a brief relationship with her, but she broke it off last week."

"Sexual?"

"Close…but never quite got that far."

"Thanks for being up front."

"You're not a damned bit welcome and I resent your asking."

"As you must know, Mr. Samuelson, we've been attempting to contact you for some time. When we've called, the person at the Samuelson College desk has repeatedly told us that you were out of town…unavailable. It wasn't until we got a subpoena and examined your agendas and travel expense reports that we learned the truth. You were in town when the three murders occurred. And you were in town when we called for an interview on five occasions. Would you care to explain?"

"What's to explain? Pretty obvious, isn't it? I didn't want to see you."

"Delay the inevitable and elevate our suspicions? Very stupid for an educated man."

"Thanks…for the educated part, but I don't fall for sucker salve. I know what I am. Don't be condescending."

"Take my comment any way you like. One bit of advice, though, which you'd better take to heart. Don't drag an innocent kid into your evasions. The campus operator could be charged for impeding our investigation."

"I suppose you've warned her not to be a bad girl again."

I didn't answer him. "Finally…for the record…would you be willing to submit to a polygraph examination?"

"Of course. Where do I sign up?"

"Will you be available tomorrow or Friday? Which day would you prefer?"

"Friday would be best…if I really have a choice."

"Any particular time?"

"No…only not too early. I don't get up until nine. Ten would be fit my schedule fine…if you give a damn, which you probably don't."

"Would you mind waiting while I schedule the exam?"

"No problem, Detective. What's another wasted half hour?"

When I returned from scheduling the polygraph exam, Dustan had his feet on the table. A cigarette was hanging from his mouth in violation of Florida law against indoor smoking.

"The smoke, Mr. Samuelson. You're violating state law."

"Sure, Mister detective. Anything to please. After taking his feet from the table, he removed the cigarette from his mouth and snuffed it out on the varnished

table top and smirked, "Am I legal now, detective...
what's your name?"

"Brad Paxton," I said. "We'll continue this interview
after we have the results of the polygraph...uh...what
was your name, sir?"

* * *

Nan and I got together after the departure of Dustan and Nina. After listening to the taped interviews,
we discussed our reactions. My summary of Nina's
interview was simple and general. "Nina Samuelson is
scared to death of her husband. She's under his thumb
big time." Nan agreed that my take was consistent with
hers.

Nan's reaction to my interview with Dustan was
explicit. "The man sounds like a borderline sociopath.
He's one arrogant s.o.b....very certain he can beat a
polygraph...and he probably will. One other thing, I
believe Hernando had better watch his back. You don't
put this guy down and get away with it. I think we'd better talk to the Lieutenant about his beautiful nephew's
safety." I agreed except for the "beautiful" part. I'd have
said "handsome".

28

We hit the highlights of our interviews with Dustan and Nina Samuelson with the Lieutenant. Then we requested some help. We'd agreed--Nan and I—that we should put a tail on Dustan, Jr.

"You really believe he's that dangerous?" the Lieutenant asked.

"You tell us after you listen to the tape."

"Later. I'll do the tape tonight. But if you're that damned sure that the man's dangerous, I'll shake someone loose. One of our more nondescript types," Luis said.

"Not too nondescript," Nan said, "he could end up as the subject of our next embalming."

"How about Chews?" I said. The reference was to Detective Arnold Czewieski, a tall, disjointed man in the mold of a latter day Ichabod Crane. Despite his ungainly appearance and languid demeanor, intelligence wise, Chews had a chain-saw mind that could tear through the convoluted verbiage of our less gifted detectives.

"You like Chews, don't you, Rock? Most of the guys steer clear of him…except when on a case."

"Chews is brighter than I am or ever will be, and I don't allow it to bother me. Some of the guys don't like a man who can rip one of their half-assed theories into shreds in a whisper."

"I think you've got it right, Rock. Despite getting straight A's in elementary school, I find the man somewhat intimidating." Luis smiled and tapped his forehead. I wondered why he was in such a good mood. I found out later he'd won twenty dollars on a state lottery scratch off.

"Okay Einstein. Do we get Chews?" I said.

"Okay with you, Nan?" Luis asked

"Why not. I'm just a lowly woman. I don't have to compete with you gifted males. I think Chews is cute," she said.

"I'll get Chews and Hernando in for a briefing. Make yourselves available this afternoon. Okay?"

"You're the boss, Lieutenant. We'll hang around."

* * *

From his Lexus, Dustan Samuelson eyed the area around the Ybor City Campus of Hillsborough community college. The parking lot was half empty. In a half hour, the last evening class would be over. And only a few vehicles would remain. A few faculty would stay behind along with the night maintenance crew.

He noticed a skinny guy sitting on a bus stop bench eating an ice-cream cone. The man got up and walked into the darkness. A car left. Another pulled in and parked with its engine running, parking lights on. Waiting for someone. A spouse. A sibling. A lover. A friend.

A patrol car pulled up behind him, headlights blinking. He was blocking the alley. Cursing, he pulled into the street. He waved at the men in the patrol car and they waved back. "Bastards," he muttered. He circled the block and returned to his spot in the alley.

He drummed the dashboard with his fingertips. Tiring of that, he ran his fingers over the 38 caliber Smith and Wesson snub-nosed revolver that lay on the seat beside him. He picked it up, hefted it, put it back on the set. Georgia came into view and walked toward her car.

She wasn't his target. Not tonight, but she owed him, and she would eventually pay her debt. After she drove off, he opened the door of his Lexus. When her lover boy left the building and entered the parking lot, Dustan had crossed the narrow street and taken a position in the shadow of one of the few remaining vehicles. He knew where Hernando had parked. He'd been watching when the lean Latino arrived for his class. His two-hour wait was almost over. Almost. He licked his dry lips and sighted his weapon on Hernando's chest as he walked toward him.

He tightened his grip on the weapon and damned his sweaty palms. When Hernando reached a point two car lengths away, he squeezed the trigger, the gun bucked, and the target was no longer there.

"Okay, jerk. Target practice is over. Drop your damned weapon." The firm order came from behind, and somehow he knew that the lean guy with the ice cream cone had been waiting for him.

Furious, Instead of complying with the command to drop his weapon, Dustan whirled and sank to one knee, bringing his weapon to bear on the man behind him. He had turned in the wrong direction as Chews stepped aside, and the full two pound plus weight of his gun slammed into the side of Dustan's head.

The last thing Dustan heard as he slumped forward was his assailant saying, "Hey, Hernando, come on over and help me with this guy. He's a bull."

* * *

Chews called for a backup. Within ten minutes after the call, a squad car arrived. Fifteen minutes later, Dustan Samuelson, Jr., was awake, sullen, handcuffed and having stitches taken in the two inch gash on the left side of his skull. Chews watched the repair work with a satisfied grin each time Dustan flinched.

Samuelson had already threatened to sue the department and the "skinny s.o.b." who'd slugged him, saying he was simply protecting himself from a Latin punk who had assaulted him a week earlier. He also said he had a witness to the assault, one Georgia Selby, a member of the Ybor City campus faculty.

After booking, Junior made a phone call, and then spent a full forty-five minutes in a holding cell uttering every vulgarity he'd learned on an elementary school playground with subtle variations in subject, verb tense, and object.

Dustan senior and the lawyer both arrived in rather disheveled condition. Senior had been called from bed and the lawyer from a cocktail party. The lawyer insisted on an immediate bail hearing, which he knew wasn't forthcoming. And after a short discussion with his client—to which Senior listened without comment—the duo departed with as much dignity as they could muster under the circumstances. Senior, back to bed. The attorney, back to the cocktail party and the blonde entertainer who had told him that he was cute.

* * *

Nan and I were up with the birds and in with Dustan before their first twitter.

"Got yourself in a real jam, Samuelson," I said.

"I'm not talking without my lawyer," he said.

"He's on the way."

"I'll wait."

"You realize that you attempted to kill a citizen employed by the city."

"A cop?"

"No, not a cop. But the relative of a very important cop."

"So, I'll get railroaded for protecting myself. Uh...you said 'attempted.' The pretty punk's okay?"

"Doesn't matter, does it? You're up for assault with intent to kill and stalking...since you admitted it was payback for something that happened over a week ago." A buzzer advised that the lawyer had arrived. He introduced himself as Tyrone Winkler of Winkler, Winkler, and Winkler. I was attempted to ask how Ms. Winkler was holding up, but resisted the impulse.

"You've been interrogating my client without me being here to protect him from self incrimination? This shall be part of our appeal."

"Who was interrogating your client? We have a recording that says otherwise. Unless interrogation means conversation."

"Okay," Winkler said, turned on a recorder, and indicated with a nod that we could begin..

"First. Some past business. During our last interview, yesterday morning…Mr. Samuelson…you agreed to take a polygraph…"

"Hold it, detective. I wasn't present when my client agreed to a polygraph examination...unless my memory fails me."

"Your memory's okay, counselor. The fact is he didn't request legal representation. I think he'll verify that…since we have a recording of that interview, also."

"Is the polygraph relevant to the current charges, Detective Paxton?"

"Not directly…a tangential matter."

"Tangential? Not the alleged attempt to kill a young Latin, Hernando Wright?"

"No," I said.

* * *

The interview with Samuelson continued for forty-five minutes and got nowhere beyond a claim that he'd been waiting outside the classroom building to talk to "that young Latin punk" and had taken a revolver to protect himself. He denied Chews' written report that he fired his weapon from hiding and made no effort to talk to his intended victim before doing so. We turned our recording over to an ADA who had watched the interview and had previously verified the events at the crime scene with Chews and two witnesses. He said he was prepared for the bail hearing. I expressed my delight over the fact that Dustan would have to spend the following weekend in a cell because of a backlog of bail hearings.

29

Hernando Wright pressed the doorbell and waited impatiently for Georgia to answer. He had to explain. When the door opened, he ducked a wild swing and stepped into the house.

"Hold it, Georgia. Give me a minute to explain, and I'll leave...if that's what you want."

"Why would I want you to stay, you traitorous gigolo?" He noticed that her eyes were red. She'd been crying.

"I don't blame you for being upset, kiddo. But maybe I should be a little pissed, too."

"Why you? You were spying on me. I know you're a damned undercover cop. Two of your former classmates called this morning and said they saw Dustan shoot at you and watched you fall to the ground. They thought you'd been killed…but said you stood up and took off one of those…vests…and helped another policeman put cuffs on Dustan…and…"

"All true except for one thing. I'm not a cop. My uncle is and he asked me to help the department find out what you knew about the three mortician murders…Rockefeller's murder in particular."

"What's the difference? You were working for them, spying on me. Using me."

"Seems like that worked both ways…or didn't you use me to get Dustan Samuelson out of you life? I really believe I walked into a set up that night. You on the bed screaming. Dustan standing over you like an honest to God rapist."

Georgia blushed. A small smile touched her lips. "I guess I'm a jerk. A disappointed jerk. I thought you were attracted to me…but I suppose I'm just a forty-two year old has been in your eyes."

"I'll be damned if I think you're a has been, kiddo. Remember, I saw you naked. Impressive. I think you're a very lovely woman…an exciting woman…a woman I enjoy being around."

"Do you mean that…are you being truthful or are you still working for your uncle?"

"I'd like to think I'm working for Uncle Luis and for you...working for you both."

"Can't be. He wants to send me to prison."

"And I want to prove you had nothing to do with Rockefeller's murder. Anyway, the Lieutenant wants to send whoever committed the murders to prison...not you specifically."

"You don't believe I was involved? Hold me please, Hernando. Hold me tight. I want so very much to believe in you...trust you with my life."

Hernando pulled her close and tucked his chin in her fragrant, dark hair. "I'll never deceive you again, kiddo. I won't judge you, and when you're ready to talk...I'll listen to whatever you want to tell me."

* * *

Peter Cromwell and Victor Parnell shared a table outside a Starbucks' coffee shop in Tampa International Airport's main terminal. Parnell had been waiting for the CPA when he disembarked from a DC flight.

"What's so important that it couldn't wait until tomorrow?" Cromwell said with obvious irritation.

"Dustan pulled a real piece of stupidity. I guess Selby kissed him off so he followed her home from her class a week ago last Wednesday night. The jerk didn't know that the police had an undercover man on her, and the cop shows up and beats the hell out of him…Dustan…in her house. So what does the stupid ape do? A week later, he hides behind a car in the School's parking lot and shoots the guy…out of jealousy…for God's sake."

"Was the cop killed?"

"He was wearing a Kevlar vest…anyway…another cop signaled the guy to duck when Dustan had a bead on him."

"How'd you get this inside stuff?"

"I talked to some guys I know at City Hall."

"Dustan get bail?"

"No bail hearing yet…tomorrow or day after. I…"

"Hold it, Victor. Give me some time to think."

Several minutes passed as Cromwell considered the situation created by Dustan's impetuousness. Finally, ready to present his analysis, he said, "When I asked him to keep an eye on Selby, I didn't expect him to get possessive. Anyway, it's done. Dustan isn't brilliant, but he sure as hell knows attempted murders don't carry the same penalty as successful ones. He should also realize that the payoff for keeping his mouth shut is worth a few years in prison."

"He could make a deal."

"No deal would hold up. He doesn't know anything we didn't want him to know, and anything he says can be refuted by two…no three…respectable citizens.

"What about Georgia?"

"Georgia's got the most to lose. She has to go along. The deck's stacked in our favor."

"I don't know, Peter. I don't know how you can be so damned certain everything's not about to blow up."

"I know people, Victor. We won't go down no matter what happens. Not because we all have too much to lose, but because you and I have covered our asses too well. If anyone takes a fall, it'll be Dustan and Georgia. They have a pair of treys. And we have a royal flush. They call. They lose."

"There's one player that isn't locked in. Maybe we're one card short in our flush…if you know who I mean."

"We'll have our flush when it's time for the pay-off…believe it. There will be no loose ends. A player may have to be disposed of…and as you very well know…you control the means of disposal."

30

"We got a card from Dad today. From Vienna." Midge laid the postcard on the table next to my coffee and leaned over my shoulder as I read it. The card carried a photo of the statue of Marie Theresa centered in a vast Plaza between Vienna's museums of Natural History and Art. On the reverse side was a cryptic note in Dad's hand writing. It was legible but hardly Spenserian:

Having a splendid extended honeymoon. Denise is fine. Sends her best. Tour guide said Marie Theresa had seventeen or eighteen babies. Forget which. You two have a ways to go. Better get busy. Love ya'. Dad

"Seventeen or eighteen babies? Wow. He's laid out quite a challenge," I said. "You up to it?"

"It's okay for him to say 'cause he doesn't have to carry them around for nine months," Midge said, patting her tummy. Then, because she was an ex-bank employee, she began to do some calculations. "Let's see…say she had seventeen…nine times seventeen… good Lord. That would be a total of one-hundred-and-fifty-three months of pregnancies. Which would be…twelve-and-three-quarter years. I can't believe it. She must have been a horse."

"Horse? Watch it, kid, you're talking about royalty here…big time. The Hapsburgs. Anyway, that doesn't sound so bad," I said. "Let's say the average woman lives eighty years and has her first baby at twenty… then has babies at a rate of one every twelve months. She'd have her seventeenth child at age thirty seven. She'd have the rest of her life…forty three years…to play golf, shop, nag her husband…"

"But who takes care of those kids until they all leave home? Who does the cooking, bathing, washing, ironing, shopping and all the other stuff mothers do?"

"There's a simple answer to that. You teach them self sufficiency from day one," I said, as soberly as I could. "The father would be the training supervisor. The oldest would be responsible for rearing the youngest, the second oldest, the second youngest."

"And what if they didn't achieve the required level of self sufficiency?"

"The brilliant and always prepared father would shift gears and give the responsibility to a person or persons hired to do the cooking, bathing and...what were the rest of those mundane little chores?"

"Which would...of course...give his wife time to shop, play golf and have babies. You're a nut, do you know that? A super nut." Midge wrapped her arms around my neck and did her nibbling thing, which I took as the prelude to something else she liked to do. Then the phone rang. It was the Lieutenant, calling from the golf course.

* * *

Dustan Samuelson, Senior, Nan and I were in the Lieutenant's office waiting for him to arrive. Samuelson refused to discuss what had brought him to homicide until Luis arrived. So Nan and I discussed the weather, pizza, bourbon and other such nonsense to spice up the interlude between our arrival and that of our superior. I sat in unease expecting her to bring up Georgia Selby's bon-bons at any time. I was relieved when Luis arrived, flushed and perspiring from his interrupted Saturday round of golf.

"Okay. What's up? Rock?"

"We came right down after your call saying Dr. Samuelson was here asking for you. We've been with him for a half hour, but he's refused to discuss what brought him here until you arrived. That's it."

"Doctor?"

"First...I must insist on confidentiality...insist that anything I say will not leave this room. This is very important...critically important to me and my family."

"If you're going to disclose a prosecutable crime...I can't make that promise." Luis mopped his forehead as he spoke.

"I'm not here to report a crime...just some situations that I find very troubling. I'm not an alarmist, Lieutenant, but I consider myself a perceptive man, and I've noted...perceived...an atmosphere of...how may I describe it? Fear. Yes, an atmosphere of fear...of secretive behavior...of apprehension."

"I must ask for a specific, Doctor. Who is apprehensive? Secretive?"

"My daughter, Sheri. Won't talk about Victor, Victor Parnell her husband. Leaves the college without explanation. I've had to remove her from her classes for being...well...intoxicated. She's lost weight...doesn't smile." He glanced at me with a sad smile. "A trait perfected by her father as your detective will attest. But it's not natural for her...she's always been a bright, upbeat person."

"We're not psychiatrists, Doctor. I don't know what you expect us to do."

"The truth is...I don't know how to put this...the change in her behavior started about the time those embalmed cadavers started showing up."

"You think she's involved in some way...is that it?"

He hesitated before answering. Then—while staring at the nails of his long-fingered hands--he said in a near whisper, "Yes...that is what I believe...God help me. I do love her so much...but that husband of hers...Victor...is a no-good, conniving bastard."

The man that I had labeled as cold and unemotional covered his face with his hands and shook with violent sobs. His audience of three detectives—including me, the Rock—were hoping for his sake that his lovely daughter was not involved, was not Marian.

When he removed his hands, his eyes were swollen. We rejected his apology in unison. The Lieutenant ended the session. "We will keep this discussion confidential, Doctor. You do understand that we have...for obvious reasons...been looking at Victor Parnell and your daughter in this matter. But I'll promise you this much. Your daughter shall not be subjected to any undue harassment. And no charges will be brought until we're absolutely certain that we have a case.

"I suppose…that's all I…we can expect. Thank you Lieutenant Agosto."

Part Four

From a motivational perspective, murder for financial gain seems more iniquitous, less forgivable, than murder incited by jealousy, alcohol, or misguided compassion. However, the victim is no less dead whether the murderer is a kidnapper, a drunk or a jealous lover.
CBW - 08

31

I arranged a meeting with Sheri Samuelson two days after Dr. Samuelson's visit to homicide. At her insistence, we met in her office at the college. Dr. Samuelson had been correct. His daughter was no longer the buoyant, self assured beauty I'd met several weeks earlier. She was thinner, pale and nervous. It was immediately apparent that someone or something had drained her vitality like aphids on a rose. The odor of booze reached me across the desk when she spoke. Hard stuff.

"I'm not quite certain why you've chosen to interview me about these horrible murders, Detective Paxton."

"Before we start, Ms. Parnell, do you mind if I record your responses? If I don't have to take notes, it'll speed up the process."

"I'm for whatever speeds up the process," she said and laughed. The laugh was forced. Phony.

"Good. Thank you. First, on the questionnaire my partner and I sent out, you answered in the negative regarding your willingness to submit to a polygraph examination. Is that correct?"

"Yes…it is correct."

"Is that still your position?"

"Yes."

"You realize that it could clear you of suspicion in the three murders we're investigating?"

"It could also make me appear guilty."

"Did someone tell you that?"

"Yes."

"May I ask who?"

"Why…I don't suppose she'd mind…it was Adrianna Cromwell. She teaches here part time, and we're very good friends."

"You know that she also refused the polygraph for the same reason?"

"Yes. She told me when she advised me not to do it."

"Are you aware that she and her husband are also among our prime suspects in this case?"

She stared at me before responding. Disbelief tempered by interest. "No…I wasn't aware of that."

"How well do you know Peter Cromwell?"

"We've been out together a few times…as couples."

"They seem to get along? You know…do they appear to be happily married?"

"I don't believe I care to dish out dirt about a good friend, Detective."

"Okay. I'll ask Dustan's wife…Nina"

"That will be difficult."

"Why difficult?"

"Nina has…disappeared."

"Disappeared? When?"

"She hasn't been here for three days. Dad called their place… Dustan's and hers. There's been no answer."

"Does Dustan know about her disappearance?"

"Yes. Victor visited him in jail and told him."

"Really." I glanced at Nan. She nodded. "My partner and I need to follow this up. I'll have to postpone the rest of this interview, but I have one last question for you. Do you mind?"

"No."

"How do you and Victor get along? On a scale from one to ten?"

"How do we…oh God."

"Do you have something to tell me, Sheri?" I reached across her desk and took her hand. She was trembling.

"There's nothing…I can tell you…please leave. Go find Nina. She's a sweet kid. I think something may have happened to her."

I smiled at this frightened woman as I stood to leave. I had a feeling that she also knew something about Nina's disappearance and that something might crack our case wide open.

"Look, Sheri. I know something's tearing at your psyche. You need help or it'll destroy you. Before that happens, call me. I can help you, and I want to. We can meet anywhere any time."

* * *

Nina Samuelson lay bound and gagged on a tray in the Parnell Family crematory. She was in a holding area away from the cremation chambers. Before he left her there, she had looked into Victor Parnell's eyes and saw death. Her death. There was no mercy for her in those gloating, laughing eyes. She'd known him since he and Sheri had married, but she'd never seen the monster in him. She had one chance of leaving the crematory alive. He had explained that to her in very concise terms:

"If your beloved, stupid husband accepts his punishment like the man he isn't, you'll be released with enough money to return to Bogota where he found you whoring. If he talks…the flames in a chamber on the other side of that wall will devour you with all the information the stupid bastard gave you."

She knew a promise not to tell him what she'd learned from her imprisoned husband would do no good. No. Her only hope was that Dustan would not make a deal, but she had no confidence that he wouldn't. She also realized that—from what she knew—Peter Cromwell and Victor Parnell were well insulated against discovery and prosecution because of her husband's stupidity. His greed.

* * *

A cooperative Dr. Samuelson set up interviews with the staff and faculty of his College. Gave us a two rooms to conduct interviews and also provided a schedule and a gofer to execute the schedule. After five hours of interviews, Nan and I got together and compared notes. We didn't have much to compare. However, two things seemed consistent and a third very important: Most of the staff didn't care for Dustan Jr.; most liked Nina; and the last time anyone saw Nina she was in the staff parking lot talking to Victor Parnell. This meeting had been observed by three staff members on a break and had occurred the day Nina Samuelson disappeared.

Nan and I went to Dr. Samuelson's office to thank him for his assistance with the interviews.

"I was glad to help, Detectives. Something evil is destroying my daughter. And now something has happened to that sweet kid, Nina...Dustan's wife. I believe there's a connection."

On the possibility he'd offer something of value, I asked, "Do you have any idea what that connection would be, Doctor?"

He didn't hesitate. "Victor," he said. I believe my son is in jail because of some sort of relationship with Victor. And I also believe Victor is destroying my daughter. The self-centered bastard."

"Obviously, you don't care for Victor, Doctor,."

"Never have. Never trusted him, and I didn't want Sheri to marry him...but..." He shrugged and broke off his comments about his son-in-law. Extending his hand, he said, "God be with you, detectives. I hope you find Nina...and you discover the cause of my daughter's debilitation." I looked at Nan and felt that she and I were thinking the same thing: love of his daughter had exposed the human side of the doctor. A side that had escaped me on our first meeting.

32

At four o'clock, Nan and I arrived back in the squad room and were met by Chews. It was a surprise. We thought he'd gone on to other assignments.

"Chews. Damn…are you still with us?"

"The Lieutenant thinks I might be helpful on this mortician thing. He's been getting some crap from on high. So I've been nosing around and got some stuff that might interest you."

"Shoot, friend."

"Hernando and I had a long conversation…you know he's still hanging out with that Selby lady, and she knows he was working undercover for the Lieutenant."

"Why's he still hanging out with her if his cover's blown?" Nan asked, beating me one more time.

"Two reasons. First, he likes her...a lot. I actually think he loves her, but is afraid of the word 'love'. Been a bachelor so long he's afraid there are wedding bells associated with saying you're in love. And second... and more to the point...he believes she can deliver on the murders. But she's scared to death of person or persons as yet unnamed. Based on a ton of conversation with her, he's certain she's being blackmailed to keep her mouth shut about the Rockefeller murder. He thinks she's very close to confiding in him."

"I sure as hell hope he's right," I said. "Anything else, Chews?"

"Yeah. Coupla' things. The Rockefeller will is scheduled for probate next week. Good possibility it'll bring a snake or two out of the rocks when the money's freed up."

"And?"

"Victor Parnell visited Dustan Samuelson three days ago. We might want to go see our little jailbird."

"Three days ago? The day Nina disappeared?" I said. "Nan, why don't you and Chews visit Dustan... see if he'll open up about Parnell's visit."

"And what will you be doing?" Nan asked,

"Visiting Parnell at his barbecue pit...see if he may be planning to destroy some important evidence."

"Take Chews," Nan said. "I can handle Dustan… there's built in backup at the jail…you know…bars, bells and whistles and a ton of guards. Take Chews. I also suggest you get a search warrant."

* * *

A cooperative jurist had us on the road fifteen minutes after an ADA explained the circumstances supporting our request. We arrived at the crematory at five thirty. There was a car our front, which we assumed was Victor's. The door was locked. We pressed a buzzer under a bronze plate that said "For Night Attendant." There was no response. I broke the glass with the butt of my weapon, and Chews and I scrambled into the foyer with our weapons drawn.

Victor Parnell appeared through a door at the rear of the foyer His face said it all. He offered a stuttered objection.

"What the hell…what right do…" I grabbed the front of his shirt and shoved the search warrant in his face.

"Here's what gives us the right. Chews, take care of Mr. Parnell while I look around."

"You can't go back there," Parnell said feebly. I noticed a growing stain on the front of his trousers.

"Like hell, I can't," I said and shoved him in Chews' direction.

I entered the room where the cremations took place. One of three stacked chambers was on. An empty lift sat in from of that chamber. I was perspiring…feeling that we were too late. That the remains of sweet little Nina Samuelson were already in a jar someplace…or scattered to the four winds or to the one wind that was coming in from the bay.

I went through a door at the back of the room. It was cool—not cold—and there she was. In a container used for cremation. Bound and gagged. I fumbled with the binding, took out my handy dandy Swiss pocket knife, and cut her free. She was in my arms sobbing hysterically as I removed the tape from round her head.

"You're okay, kid. You're all right. Safe now"

"Thank you…thank you…he was going to….oh my God. I cried. I begged God. He answered. I was so afraid."

I carried Nina into the foyer. I smiled. "We got here in time, Chews. The bastard had a cremation chamber fired up."

"Thank the Lord."

"Didn't know you were religious, friend."

"I've had my doubts. But not now. Not ever again." He looked into Nina's tear-stained face, and he said, "I'll carry this pretty little lady to the vehicle if you want to knock the living crap out of this…piss ant."

* * *

After his booking, Victor asked for a lawyer. Joker that I am, I told him he needed a magician. When he asked for dry trousers, we handed him the standard issue. A pair of orange coveralls.

He was taken to a holding cells to await his lawyer while Nan and I took Nina to another room. Obviously, we needed to learn the circumstances surrounding her trip to the crematory. Whether she'd gone with Victor willingly or under duress.

"So, Victor said that Sheri was meeting you after work to have dinner?"

"Yes. That's what he said."

"And you believed him?"

"I must have…I went with him."

"What reason did he give for meeting at the Crematorium?"

"Said he had some things to take care of there… and we'd be closer to the restaurant. Said it was just a matter of convenience."

"Do you like Victor?"

"Thought he was okay before...now...I hate him. He's a creep...creepy."

"After you got there...what happened?"

"He asked if I'd ever seen...a cremation chamber."

"And?"

"I said I hadn't and didn't care to...see one."

"How'd he take that?'

"He laughed and grabbed my arm. I got scared then...tried to resist. He dragged me into that room... where you found me. He got me on the floor and sat on me while he tied me up. Oh...God...I was so scared...could hardly breathe."

Nan put her arms around the emotionally exhausted woman. "Okay, honey, try to relax. I think Detective Paxton only has a few more questions. Okay?"

"Okay. I'm okay."

"More than okay. You're a brave kid," I said. "Did Victor say why he was...uh...detaining you?"

"He...said...he said if Dustan kept his mouth shut... I'd be given enough money to return to Bogota where Dustan found me."

"He didn't say that you should keep quiet about Dustan's relationship with him....or anyone else?"

"No. He didn't say that."

"Are Dustan and Victor close? Good Friends?"

"They get along. I don't believe they think of each other as friends."

"What do you think of Sheri Samuelson?"

"I love her. She is a very sweet person. Very considerate. Loves animals. We share that love...of animals."

"Do you know what's wrong with Sheri?"

"What's wrong?"

"Come on, Kid. If you're close to her, you must have noticed the change in her."

"Yes, I've noticed...but I don't know anything specific... except she's very afraid of Victor. I think she hates him, also."

33

The day following our interrogations of Victor Parnell and Nina, we met in the squad conference room. There were five of us: Nan and I; Chews; Hernando Wright; and the Lieutenant. The Lieutenant kicked things off as usual. Protocol was everything.

"Okay, men...er...detectives, let's recap the situation. Delacorte and Paxton...we've got two of your original suspects locked up. Neither is talking, which is wise from their perspective. Three counts of murder added to the current charges wouldn't help their situations much. Comments?"

"I'd like to comment, Lieutenant," I said.

"You're on."

"First, my partner and I believe it's possible that Sheri Parnell or Nina Samuelson participated in the murders without being privy to the underlying motive. However, follow-up interviews with both wives produced nothing worth talking about. I thought Nina Samuelson would spill her guts...after she was within minutes of being toast. But she's still too terrified to talk...perhaps too afraid of someone we don't have in lockup. Yet."

"And you...I suspect...have a good idea who that someone is?"

"I do. We believe the top man of this whole gambit is Peter Cromwell. We both think he ordered Parnell to cremate Nina Samuelson...to keep her mouth shut. Maybe he thought she knew more than she does. We also believe he cut Dustan out of the loop after the stupid bastard tried to hit Hernando."

"We have all these 'we believe' and 'we thinks' but what do you know for certain? Or is that expecting too much? You don't know who actually embalmed our three victims as of now. Right? You don't know for sure what part Georgia Selby..."

"May I say something?" Hernando interrupted the Lieutenant.

"How can I deny my favorite nephew the floor? Go."

"I've gotten very close to Ms. Selby over the past few weeks. Close enough…that I don't believe she'd lie to me. She insists that she had nothing to do with Rockefeller's murder. She was getting along fine… didn't need his money. Liked the little guy. Thought of him as a friend. She says he actually told her if she ever needed help, he'd give what she needed."

"What else do you expect her to say? She knows about your ties to the department." Chews said. I had a feeling that the angular man was doing more than trying to put Hernando on the spot.

"She's also terrified. I think…excuse me Lieutenant…I think someone has her on a short leash, and until that person is locked up…" Hernando shrugged.

"You think she'd talk if offered protective custody?" Chews asked.

"She might…I don't know. I could ask."

"Why don't you," Chews said. "I'd be happy to share the baby sitting for the pretty lady with you after I get clearance from the wife. Lieutenant says okay, I'll take days and you can have nights. I suspect you know your way around Georgia's place in the dark pretty well by now."

* * *

The meeting lasted another hour. As I drove home afterward, I had this feeling that I was overmatched. As I said at the meeting, my gut told me Peter Cromwell was the prime mover in the whole gambit. He was an arrogant bastard. But you can't arrest a man for attitude. Yours or his.

Who was Mort? Who was Marian? Were Mary O'Malley and Winnie Houser's murders committed to cover up the motive for Rockefeller's murder? Or Were all three committed by persons who thought they were serving a noble purpose?

My head was spinning as I entered the house, but Midge met me at the door, kissed me, and brushed my hair back. I buried my face in her hair and said, "God, how I love you, sweetheart. Every day when I come home, I realize how very much I need you…how much I miss you….how very much I love you."

"Poor baby," she said, sensing my fatigue. "Let's sit on the couch and cuddle. You can feel the baby kick if you like."

34

Two days after the team had gathered to discuss our progress—or lack of same—word came down from the prosecutor's office that Dustan Samuelson, Sr., had come to the rescue of Junior by posting the one-million dollar bond set at the bail hearing. Dustan had been placed on house arrest and was wearing an ankle bracelet. From what I knew of the father-son relationship, I assumed that Senior had exercised what he believed to be his parental responsibility. I doubted that he did it out of love. Dustan would be hard to love—easy to hate. Even for a father.

Something else about the news bothered me. Everything I knew about the man said that of all our several suspects, Dustan was the most volatile, the most likely to brood over a slight---real or imagined--until he avenged himself. I knew Hernando would be in danger as would Georgia Selby. I recalled the loathing, the seething resentment in his dark eyes and in his voice when I questioned him. I had churned up his bile. I'd seen evil in him. Hell, I could be a target, something I'd considered before that had stayed with me.

During these mental aerobics on the potential consequences of Dustan's bail out, something happened to me that had never happened before during my police career. I was frightened, not for myself, but for Midge and our baby--six months along and doing well, thank you. With this on my mind, I asked myself a series of questions: Was Dustan Samuelson, Jr., capable of a killing spree? I knew Hernando and Georgia were the most likely targets of a boil over of hate. Who else after that? Would he come after me? After my family? Nina? Perhaps, anxiety was drafting the dark images that tumbled through my mind. I knew one thing for sure. He would die if he came close to Midge. He would die in severe pain.

* * *

"What's up, partner?" Nan interrupted my ruminations by patting my head and parking her butt on the corner of my desk. Something I'd grown used to. Nan

was anything but a shrinking violet. She had flamboy-
ant tendencies.

"You heard Dustan's out on bail?" she asked

"Yeah, I heard."

"Kind jurists and generous, wealthy, and forgiving
fathers are the bane of civilized society."

"That's a rather extreme indictment of judges and
generous and forgiving fathers," I said.

"One size fits all when I see nuts like Dustan Samuelson bailed out."

"You've got a point…a dull one, though. I've been
thinking about Dustan. Wondering if he won't be more
dangerous now than he was when he tried to take out
Hernando," I said.

"Do you need to wonder? I think he's one angry animal. Seriously…aside from my prior bit of hyperbole…I
really believe Hernando, Georgia and Nina may all
need someone covering their backs until Dustan is
locked up for good."

"Now that you're being serious, do you think he
could come after me?"

"You? I hadn't thought about it. Why you?"

"He showed some real animosity toward me during my interviews with him. I can handle myself…but

I'm concerned over what might happen to Midge if he came after me at home."

"You may be wrestling with your primal nature, dear one. The inner animal seeks to protect his or her own."

"So, Doc, I've given in to a primitive instinct to protect my brood?"

"You got it. Me Tarzan. That Jane. That Boy. You hurt. I kill."

"I suppose I've overreacted."

"Maybe. But be alert, friend. You've got a broad back... big target for errant slugs. Okay. Other than that, what's on tap for today?"

"I'd like to take another shot at Sheri Samuelson. Perhaps, Victor's incarceration will eventually loosen her tongue...even though I really believe it's not Victor she's afraid of."

"You still think Cromwell's...Oh...I almost forgot. Our check of Cromwell's telephone communications came up with something very interesting."

"Yeah?"

Those trips to DC were all preceded by calls to one number in Fairfax, Virginia."

"That where his client lives?"

"Could be, but I doubt it. Calls were to a small company that does recordings, dubs tapes, produces masters....that sort of thing. Here."

Nan handed me a printout of Cromwell's out of state calls for a three month period. The Washington area calls were highlighted. There were six to the True Blue Sound Studio.

I smiled at Nan. "Let's postpone our visit to Sheri Samuelson and see if we can find out why Peter's visiting a sound studio."

35

We waited in Peter Cromwell's reception area for him to finish a call. It was a lengthy call. We'd been waiting twenty five minutes when we got permission to enter his office from his receptionist, a dowdy matron who'd undoubtedly been hired by Adrianna. The patent friendliness we'd experienced on our previous visit wasn't there. Peter had obviously decided he didn't like us very much. Of course, I didn't care much for him either.

He stood at his desk and indicated that we should sit in the office's conference corner. We accepted and occupied two of the six chairs arranged around a Maple table. Cromwell joined us.

"Detectives. I hate to hold you up, but I've advised my counsel that you were here. She's on her way and should be here shortly." We looked at each other, nodded, and waited another five or ten minutes. Cromwell had brought some paperwork with him to the table and worked while we sat. I don't think he was in the mood for idle chatter.

A buzzer rang and dowdy lady said, "Attorney Perry is here, Mr. Cromwell. Should I send her in?"

"Of course."

April entered the office smiling. She looked improved over our previous, post Sudan meetings. Much improved. After greeting us, she took a chair next to Cromwell, opened a binder, turned on a recorder, and place it beside ours. Hers looked more expensive. Then she nodded for us to begin.

"A few things we'd like clarified, Mr. Cromwell."

"Help yourself," he said with his Robert Taylor, pretty boy smile. I knew it was for Nan and April's consumption. Peter obviously liked women.

"First, we'd like your reaction to the indictment of Victor Parnell," I said.

"If what I heard is factual, he deserves whatever comes his way."

"That appears to be a rather callous comment considering that he's your friend."

"As I said...if the charges are true...I wouldn't wish to continue the friendship. I don't ordinarily socialize with criminals."

"You're not giving him the benefit of doubt...you know... innocent until proved guilty."

"Am I supposed to react to that? Was it a question?"

"Sounds like a fair weather friend to me.," Nan stuck in the needle. April objected.

"When was the last time you saw Victor?"

"I'm not certain. A few days ago."

"Could it have been the day he took Dustan's wife to the crematory?" I gave him my "All knowing, All Seeing" Karnack look. I'd been practicing in the morning when shaving. The bluff worked.

"It could have been. I arrived from DC and met him at the airport. It was just a coincidence. I believe he was picking someone up...he may have mentioned it. I can't recall."

"You just spoke in passing? Or did you take time for a drink with him? Maybe a coffee?" He was getting nervous and glanced at April repeatedly.

Finally, April asked, "Is this going somewhere, Detective Paxton?"

"Yes, counselor. We believe Victor Parnell was acting in conjunction with or on orders from a co-conspirator. We also believe that he and this other person were both involved in the so-called mortician murders. We're attempting to pin down the movements of our three primary suspects on the day Nina Samuelson was abducted. We believe our interrogation is pertinent in that regard."

"Are you comfortable with the direction of the questioning, Mr. Cromwell?" April asked.

"I...uh...I suppose. But I want to make it clear that Victor got no directions from me and that I was not involved in those three horrible murders. I'm an accountant, for God's sake."

"Yes...but according to your wife, she has trained you in embalming procedures. Isn't that true?"

"Yes. But I'm far short of being an expert."

"We realize that, Mr. Cromwell. Detective Delacorte, do you have any questions for Mr. Cromwell?"

"Yes...if I may." She smiled at Victor. He smiled back. Seemed to relax. "Your recent trips to Washington, could you tell us the purpose for those trips?"

"Well...I can't see why its important...but I was consulting on a client's problems with the IRS."

"This was an important client?"

"Of course."

"On a scale of one to ten, how important?" His face turned red. He knew.

"Actually, it was just a friend. I volunteered to help him out of a jam."

"This friend owns and operates the Trudy Blue Sound Studio, Inc. in Fairfax?"

"Yes, damn it. Counselor. I'm not going to answer any more of their stupid, non-pertinent questions."

"You have that right, Mr. Cromwell. So…it's a wrap up, detectives. Unless and until you're prepared to bring charges…which I don't feel you're prepared to do. My client won't be available for further interviews until you are ready to press charges."

April walked with Nan and I from the office. When we arrived at the parking lot behind the building, April gave me a peck on the cheek and said, "You don't like my client very much, do you, Rock?"

"Not much. Do You?"

"You won't tell on me?"

"Of course not."

"I think he's slime." She walked to her car laughing. I could tell she felt a lot better.

36

We had just cleared Cromwell's parking lot when we were jarred to attention by Nan's cell phone ringing. Actually, it was not ringing. It was playing The Boogie Woogie Bugle Boy minus the Andrews sisters. When it came to entertainment, Nan went way back. Cripes. Gams. George Raft. Boogie Woogie. I looked at her in mock disgust. She shrugged, smiled, and answered the call.

"Yes, Ms. Samuelson. Of course. We'll be right there." Nan shoved her cell into a jacket pocket. "Ms. Samuelson…Sheri's mother ….she believes something's happened to Sheri. She's at the farm and she isn't answering her phone."

"The farm? What farm?"

"Damned if I know…but we'd better find out. I have the Samuelson home address."

* * *

We arrived at the Samuelson mansion in Galbraith Isles, a swanky Tampa enclave. We didn't have to wait. Ms. Samuelson met us on the front porch. She explained that the farm was forty acres or so that Dustan Senior had purchased for Sheri when she'd graduated from college.

"Why do you believe she'd be there, Ms. Samuelson?" I asked.

"She loves the place…or she did. Originally, she'd planned on becoming a vet…starting a clinical practice and a boarding kennel …but she met Victor…"

"Can you give us directions to this farm?"

"May I go with you?"

"I don't know…" I said and looked at Nan. She nodded. "Okay…let's hit it ladies.

* * *

Bubble light on, we arrived at the farm in short order. As soon as the vehicle stopped, Ms. Samuelson was out and running toward the house. She had a set of keys and had shut off the security system and unlocked the front door before Nan and I caught up. We made a quick tour of the house and didn't find Sheri.

"She's not here," I said the obvious and looked at the distraught mother.

"The barn...she planned a lab of sorts there...I've never seen it, but she told me about her plans."

Through a rear door window, I could see a small barn. The door was open and a small Mercedes was parked inside. "Is that Sheri's vehicle?" I asked Ms. Samuelson who had joined me at the window.

"Yes...yes. That's hers." She almost fell trying to get through the door ahead of Nan and me.

I could hear an engine running as we entered the barn. A metal-clad door to the right of the vehicle was partially open. I don't believe I was surprised when we entered Mort and Marian's mortuary.

It wasn't difficult to figure out what was going on. A small gasoline engine was running. A hose connected to its exhaust ended at the bottom of a coffin-shaped plywood box. I shut down the engine.

Standing beside the box, Nan said, "Oh, my God."

Mother Samuelson shoved Nan aside, looked through the viewing port, and let out a shriek that pierced my sinuses. Nan wrapped her arms around the distraught mother. I opened the execution chamber's lid and looked down into Sheri Samuelson's lovely face. She was at peace. She was wearing a simple white dress. In her slender hands she held a small bouquet of wild flowers. Two sealed envelopes lay at her side. One addressed to her mother. The other to Detective Rock Paxton. To me.

* * *

We contacted the Sheriff's office and waited. When the county boys arrived, we asked for and got an agreement to allow our forensics people to work with theirs on the crime scene investigation.

Before all of the evidence collection and cataloging was complete, Nan and I had toured the farm, experienced the beauty of Sheri Samuelson in the well maintained canine graveyard with its small white grave markers, and many flower beds.

After I read Sheri's note, I knew who Mort and Marian were for sure. And I came away believing that Sheri Samuelson's greatest sin had been marrying a man who had no soul:

Dear Detective Paxton,

I'm so sorry that I've taken a coward's way out, but I couldn't keep my horrible secret any longer. I accept my part in the murders of William Rockefeller, Mary O'Malley, and Winnie Houser. I allowed Victor to play on my love for him and my misguided compassion. I was stupid. Really. And I never thought of myself as a stupid person. I regret the pain my acts and my death will cause my dear mother and father. I have prayed over my sin and go to my death believing that a merciful God will be inclined to forgive a fool who was deceived into believing she was doing a good thing.   Sheri Samuelson

PS – I believe Victor was involved in some sort of a scam with Peter Cromwell. They were very close and met often. I have no idea what was going on between them. I'm sorry I couldn't get up the nerve to talk to you about all of this. I liked you. Good luck in getting to the bottom of the whole mess. Your partner said that your wife is pregnant. I'm sure you'll have a beautiful child. Pray for me. I need all of the help I can get.

37

In the letter to her parents--among other personal things, which shall remain personal here—Sheri asked to be buried in the canine cemetery on the farm. She also asked that the farm be maintained as a pet cemetery to be operated by a foundation established through the use of her assets—which were substantial--and any funds her parents and friends wished to add. She directed that the mortuary be converted to a veterinary clinic, specializing in canines.

I attended the funeral service and the interment. Afterwards, Doctor Samuelson took me aside and showed me a rendering of the monument that would mark her grave: A white marble figure of a young, seated woman holding a spaniel pup in her arms.

"It's beautiful, Doctor," I said as I placed my hand on his shoulder.

"She was a beautiful person, Detective Paxton. A good person," he said. "Despite what that bastard caused..." He shrugged and wiped his eyes.

"I know she was beautiful, Doctor. She left this note for me. I'll keep the original as a reminder that some evil doers are not inherently evil people," I said and handed him a copy of Sheri's note to me. "Give my best to Ms. Samuelson. She had a horrible shock...I wish it could've been avoided."

"So do I. She won't recover quickly...neither will I. She was the beautiful side of our existence. Some don't realize that our business is essentially depressing. The only thing that makes it worthwhile is helping families overcome the grief that comes with the passing of a loved one. And...to be totally honest...I believe the whole process is overdone. Pagan."

He left me with that admission, a sad smile, and a firm hand shake. He joined his wife. As I walked away, I saw Dustan Samuelson, Jr., accompanied by a uniformed officer. An escort. They were standing in the rear circle of mourners. Dustan stared at me and smiled. It was a mocking smile. An evil smile. He didn't like me much. I knew that for sure when he offered the famed middle finger salute and threw me a kiss. I recalled that the Mafioso Dons were reputed to plant kisses on the cheeks of men marked for death. I discarded the thought. Momentarily.

* * *

We met in an interview room with Victor Parnell and his attorney John Winkler of Winkler, Winkler and Winkler. I fought an impulse to wink at Winkler. There were three of us representing the good guys: Nan and I and ADA Winnie Adkins.

Recorders on, I started. "You have been informed of the death of your wife, Sheri Samuelson?"

"Yes," he said. Staring at the table top.

"And you refused to attend the services?"

"Yes."

"Do you know that she wrote a letter admitting you and she murdered and embalmed three persons... specifically Mary O'Malley, William Rockefeller, and Winnie Mae Houser?"

"I expected that.."

"Do you admit to your participation in these murders?"

"Other than your note, what evidence do you have that my client participated in these crimes," Attorney Winkler broke in. He had to say something futile.

"I can advise you that we have sufficient evidence to add three murder counts to the current charges against your client," ADA Adkins said.

"Okay. What do you want from my client?" Winkler asked, without asking Adkins to review the evidence. The ADA looked at me and nodded. I took over.

"We know that he was a participant to the extent that he personally executed the three victims. But we believe that the motive for Billy Rockefeller's murder was for a portion of his fortune and that others were involved. We need Mr. Parnell's testimony to confirm the identity of the others and tell us how they contributed."

"How will my client benefit if he testifies? Will you take the death penalty off the table?" Counselor Winkler asked.

"Be hard to justify for someone who committed three murders, kidnapping and arrested making preparations for a fourth murder. However, I will consult with the DA," Adkins said.

"So, as you see it, it's probable that my client shall be denied sentencing consideration if he testifies? What does he get out of cooperating?"

"What he gets is knowing that the person or persons who set up the whole thing won't get away with it," I said. "We believe we know who his associates were, but we need his confirmation to act on what we believe," I said.

Victor shrugged and looked at Winkler. "Let's wait to see what the DA offers."

* * *

Nan and I sat at her desk going over the evidence we had on Peter Cromwell, Georgia Selby, and Dustan Samuelson. We didn't have much.

"Unless Victor opens up, the brains of this whole setup may skate…at least for awhile. We need a breakthrough," I said.

"Do you believe Victor will give us what we need?"

"I'd take three to one odds he will. He's a mean-spirited little bastard. I can't see him taking the fall for the people who used him for the dirty work."

My phone rang. It was Midge. "Your Dad and Denise are home," she said.

"How does he seem? Unwound? Tired?" I asked.

He's lost weight and he's talking about buying back the company. Says a clause in the sales agreement allows him to do so within one year of the sale date."

"That's good news. But I sort of expected it. How's my cute little incubator doing? Oh…did you tell Dad about the results of the sonogram?"

"Yes…and he was thrilled. Said we needed another pretty little girl in the family. By the way, I don't like being called an incubator. I hope I mean more to you than that."

"Sorry, sweetheart. I'll apologize on my knees when I get home." I knew she was becoming sensitive, which I suppose is normal for a woman in the latter stages of a pregnancy. One of us would have to cope. I knew who it would be. What then hell, I love her.

"When are you leaving?"

"Right now…sweetheart. See you in twenty…traffic permitting." I hung up. Nan was staring at me.

"You should be ashamed."

"For calling Midge my little incubator?"

"Well…that too…but for not telling your partner the sex of her Godchild….if you ask…pal."

38

I was halfway home when Nan called. Dustan Samu-elson had assaulted his police escort, stolen the man's weapon, and left him dying in the driveway of the home he shared with Nina. She was okay. Dustan had also disabled the tracking device on his ankle. No one had a clue as to his whereabouts. I believed I knew. He had shot an officer and had nothing to lose. He wouldn't do the obvious thing first. Hit Georgia and Hernando. I asked myself one question before stick-ing the bubble light on the dash and ramming the ac-celerator to the floor: Who would be the third option on his hit list?

I cut five minutes off my normal travel time. From two blocks away, I saw the flashing lights of several ve-hicles. A block away, I recognized a medic ambulance and three patrol cars. A second ambulance waited in the street in front of the house. Heart slamming my ribs, I hit the brakes and slid past the patrolman assigned to traffic control. He got to me as I climbed from my vehicle.

"Who the hell you think you are? Didn't you see me holding up my hand…"

"Look, friend…I'm Detective Rock Paxton, Tampa Police. I live here, and seeing that ambulance in my driveway scares the crap out of me…so if you don't move…"

"Okay, Detective…sorry. I get the message."

There was a covered body on the driveway. I froze in place. Couldn't walk. "God, no. Please not Midge. Please, not Midge. Then I saw her standing with Denise, Mary Jane, and Antonia. They were huddled together on a strip of grass beside the house. Staying out of the way. Midge saw me coming and moved toward me. I grabbed her and held her for a moment before I asked, "What happened? Where's Dad? How are you…the others? Cool cop me. Running off at the mouth." I stopped jabbering and waited for answers.

As I held Midge and struggled for composure, the ambulance in the driveway pulled away, lights flashing and its horn crushing the silence of the quiet neighborhood where I'd been born. A second ambulance rolled in to take the body lying under the court.

I felt Midge squirm in my grip. I was crushing her. She smiled. And took a deep breath when I released her and waited.

"Your Dad was shot, sweetheart. But the medic's said he'd be fine. He has a shoulder wound, but no broken bones."

"He was in the ambulance that just left?"

"Yes. Shouldn't we take Denise and go to the hospital…he'll be in St. Joseph's emergency room."

"I'll have to clear it with those guys," I said pointing to three plain clothes detectives who were watching a crime scene team work over the area. "Have they interviewed you yet?"

"No…should we wait and let you go on ahead?" Midge asked.

"I'm sure they'll want to interview you. I'm surprised they haven't started yet, but they're county guys and could be waiting for some preliminary stuff from the crime scene team. I'll check…see if they can speed it up."

I introduced myself and shook hands with the lead detective who introduced himself as Toad Fogarty. He was a tough-looking guy—almost as wide as he was tall, but he wasn't fat. Fogarty said he'd prefer to get a statement from Midge before she went anywhere. He was almost apologetic. I told him I understood. This was after I explained who I was and why I was there, and after I went over TPD's interest in what had occurred.

As I was leaving, Fogarty and the other two men were following Midge, Denise, Mary Jane and Antonia into the house. I could almost hear Midge saying, "It's so hot out here, could you do it in the house? I'll make some tea."

* * *

"You what?" I said, staring into Dad's smiling face. He was sitting up in bed, his left arm in a sling.

"You hard of hearing, son. I said I killed the punk. I was in the library with Denise picking out a book. We heard Midge yell…from the kitchen. I went to see what happened. I got as far as the kitchen door and heard this guy tell her to keep her mouth shut or he'd…blow her head off. Said he was going to kill her anyway when you got home. Wanted you to see him do it. Well…I sneaked up behind him, but he heard me coming and turned around and fired his weapon. Hit me in the left shoulder. He ran for the door…oh I was carrying one of your bats...I took a big one handed swing and knocked him half way out of the kitchen. Bastard had the guts of a canary. He ran out the door. I grabbed him from the rear and we both went down in the driveway. We were kind of wrestling around and the damned gun went off. He grunted. I climbed off him and he was blowing red bubbles. Called me dirty words before joined his ancestors."

"I'll be damned," I said. "You could be dead, you know."

"That's all the thanks I get? If I didn't stop him, you, Midge and my granddaughter could be dead. Maybe you, too."

I smiled and said, "I always knew you were a brave, tough guy, but I never thought I'd be thanking you for saving my life."

"What are fathers and grandfathers for?" he said.

39

I arrived via taxi at the Truly Blue Sound Systems, Inc. in Fairfax Virginia at ten the morning after Dustan Samuelson died in our driveway. It was a small shop on a sloping street that ended at the Potomac River. In antique gold letters, the proprietor's name was prominently displayed on the front door: Trudy Mansfield.

I entered the shop and pressed a buzzer that brought a smiling woman with a little gray in her brown hair. She was tall and I could see her playing beach volley ball in her prime. She had that sort of build.

"You're Ms. Mansfield?"

"Sure am. What can I do for you, sailor?"

I showed her my shield and said, "I'm from Tampa, Florida, ma'am."

"Where else?" she said, suddenly appearing deflated. Very tired. "This is about, Bill Smith, isn't it?"

"Bill Smith?"

"Yeah. Me, too. I thought the name was phony. Handsome guy about your height with a great smile. Twenty years ago I'd have pulled him down behind the counter."

"Sounds like my man. Name doesn't fit. Description does. I'm more interested in what business he had here...eleven-hundred miles from home."

"I'll be up front with you detective. I'm not looking for trouble. He came to me...four and a half months ago. Offered me three grand to do a job I'd have done for five hundred under normal conditions."

"What was the job?"

"Gave me seven recordings and had me create a single recording out of bits and pieces from each."

"Asked you to take several recordings and create a single recording of...what?"

"Straight out? A woman named Georgia buying the murder of a guy named William Rockefeller from an unnamed seller."
"Why'd you do it?"

"Business was down. He told me it was sort of a joke on this lady friend of his. I wanted to believe it."

"So, on the original recordings you used, did Ms. Selby actually arrange a hit on Rockefeller?"

"Hell no. It took a lot of imagination to give him what he wanted."

"Do you have the original recordings?"

"Sure do. Kept them in the event a handsome detective from Tampa came asking."

* * *

Everyone smiled after I played the dubbed recording and the originals. Hernando seemed particularly pleased as did Chews. They both had gotten very close to Georgie girl.

"I got a positive ID of Peter Crowell from the sound studio proprietor. I sent her a photo array with six guys via fax. She picked Peter...no doubt in her mind."

"Will she testify?"

"Yes. Said she could use a couple of days in the sunshine."

"It's that time. Go to the DA with what you have and then pick him up."

"Could we hold up on that ,"I said. "There's something that's been bothering me. I like to check it out."

"Damn, Rock. This wraps the whole thing up," the Lieutenant said.

"Please go with me, Lieutenant. Hold off forty-eight hours."

* * *

My first call was with Victor and Counselor Winkler in the lockup.

"The DA says no dice, Victor. Your best hope is that we'll drop the death penalty during the fifteen or so years of appeals."

Victor shrugged. "So, where are we…oh…I heard your old man killed Dustan."

"It was sort of an accident. But yes. Saved my butt."

"Whatever."

"Have you decided yet…about giving up Cromwell? I'd hate to see him skate. I wouldn't think you'd want him to."

"Okay. I'll give you what you want." And he did.

* * *

Nan and I picked up Peter Cromwell. He was mad as hell until I told him that his Fairfax connection had outed him. had given me copies of all his recordings and a positive ID. Then he wilted.

"She said she'd destroy the recordings."

"You want to hear them? Prove I have them?"

"No."

"Well…we have the whole story from Victor. He'll testify. So will Trudy Mansfield…woman from the recording studio. I'll go over the scenario as Victor laid it out. You can refute or clarify his story when I'm finished"

Then I went over Victor's story:

"Victor tells it this way. He took a class from Georgia Selby, and she came on to him. They started seeing each other. One night, she told him about Rockefeller's wealth after which he told you, his big buddy. A couple of days later, you came to him with a plan…a plan that you said would mean a few million for each of you out of Selby's inheritance. Then you asked Victor to introduce you to Georgia. He did as requested. and moved on to do the Mortician murders in a sequence which you prescribed. Then you took Georgia on a merry ride, leading her into discussions that you could use to create a recording wherein she asked someone to kill William Rockefeller. Victor swore that you were the mastermind. One other thing, you promised Dustan a piece of the pie if he'd keep an eye on Selby, which…quoting Victor… 'the stupid jerk screwed up big time.' "

Peter had listened intently as I went over Victor's description of the plot to blackmail Georgia Selby. When I finished, he had a question.

"I didn't kill anyone. Can the death penalty be set aside in my case."

"Cripes. You planned the whole thing, Cromwell. How can you expect to avoid the needle?" Nan asked.

"Victor doesn't know it all. I do. Someone else... a lot smarter than I am...was the brains."

"Can you prove what you're saying?"

"I can help you prove it," he said.

40

It was a dark place, a small upscale bar designed to offer its prominent clientele expensive cocktails, dainty snacks, and much privacy. Trysts with individuals other than one's spouse were common. Meetings between parties who had secrets to share with each other, but not with the press or law enforcement types were also common. No one entered who wasn't a member or who wasn't with a member. To assure that, a block of a man who'd forgotten how to talk sat in the small foyer and checked ID's.

Peter Cromwell was a member. His guest wasn't. Two shades in a rear corner booth, they were insulated from view by a heavy drape.

"So, why the meeting, Peter? I thought it was agreed there'd be no meetings until the deal with Selby was completed."

"I'm concerned about Victor...now that Sheri's dead. I'm afraid he'll tell all."

"I've talked to him several times since he's been locked up. He's vowed he'll keep quiet if we stand by the deal. I believe him."

"I wish I were as certain. His screw-up is what put him in jail."

"How's that?"

"He met me at the airport...concerned about Dustan shooting that cop. We talked about loose ends. I told him he had the means to take care of any problem. He said that he understood...so he picks up Dustan's wife to incinerate...I was referring to his wife...Sheri. I heard she was shaky, and she sure as hell was."

"Perhaps you should have used the name of the person you wanted taken out."

"I'm not going to accept the blame for his screw-up. He understood from the beginning that if he couldn't control Sheri, he'd have to dispose of her. She was the weak link. Everyone involved knew that."

"Take it easy, Peter. Everything's still on target...the way it was planned, right? You still have the goods on

Selby...the tape that says she bought a murder. As far as the cops know, Victor and Sheri believed they were performing a noble service. We're the only ones who know anything different for certain."

"Okay. I feel some better after talking about it. But I'll feel better when the whole gambit is wrapped up."

"Just play it like it was set up. We'd better break this off. I'll leave first as always. You mind paying the tab, Peter? I'll get it after the payoff."

After his guest left, Peter Cromwell said into his button mike, "I assume you've heard enough. I'm coming out."

* * *

We met Peter Cromwell outside the bar after his guest left with a tail. Chews. Peter looked around and saw only the van we'd used to monitor his conversation. No other vehicles.

"You didn't pick him up. Why the hell not?"

"To be totally honest, Peter, I don't believe we've gotten the whole story yet. We'll sweat your little friend and eventually get it all. But we'd prefer to get it from you. Simplify things, you know," I said.

"You're crazy, Paxton. You heard the man. That's all there is."

ADA Adkins, who was with us, spoke up. "I believe we can take the death penalty off the table...for you only. But If you don't pony up..."

"Okay. Okay. I swore I never would...but okay. I really didn't expect Dan to show up...but here's the story...""

* * *

We explained to Cromwell what we expected from him. Afterward, we followed him home. Closely. We watched him enter the house that he shared with Adrianna. Then we listened as we were wont to do when someone was wearing a wire for us.

"Did you meet with Uncle Dan? Yes. And you feel better about everything?"

"Not really."

"What's wrong, lover? Same old complaint?"

"Yes. Why must I use a middle man to converse with my wife anywhere but here at home? It's stupid. You don't need a layer of insulation between us. No one can put you in the mix except Dan and me. And you know I wouldn't give you up. And dear Uncle Dan thinks you're a genius. He sure as hell won't talk."

"No, he wouldn't. In fact, no one can tie Dan or me to any of this...only you. And we would both say we knew nothing about your criminal activities." Adrianna smiled and fluffed her hair.

"So, I'm set to take the fall? I face murder charges when all I did was follow your instructions….coordinate the frame of Selby… and bring Parnell and Samuelson into the mix."

"You've got to understand, Peter. I Love Uncle Dan. He's been my father since dad died. You…although I've enjoyed you at times…you are expendable."

"Expendable?"

"Deflating, isn't it? Actually, I went into this with that in mind. Put you up front…something you've always enjoyed…and let you take the fall if things didn't go according to plan."

"You heartless bitch. Damn you."

"You don't love me any more, darling? I' m hurt."

"Hurt? Damn you, you'll be hurt more when I refuse to complete arrangements for a fund transfer with Selby."

"Oh, I meant to tell you. Dan talked to sweet Georgia earlier today, and by now she's transferred five million to a numbered account in the Grand Caymans. I'll be checking on that in the morning. By the way, in the morning, I'll also be reporting to the police that you've left town."

"I'm not going anywhere," Peter said.

"Really?'" She smiled and raised her voice. "Uncle Dan, come and dispose of this pathetic creature in the hole we had dug this morning."

Dan Shepherd walked into the room holding a very large revolver. "Come along, Peter, like the good fellow you are. Hurry it up."

* * *

Nan stuck the talking end of her weapon in Dan Shepherd's ear when he walked from a door at the rear of the funeral home. "Drop your piece on the ground, Danny Boy, and then get on your belly while we shackle those bad little hands of yours. Don't hesitate. I can be a mean bitch. Right Chews?"

"A real mean bitch."

While Nan and Chews took care of Dan Shepherd, I entered the room where Adrianna Cromwell had disrobed for her nightly soak. I was accompanied by two uniformed officers. Safety concerns dictated that we not give her the courtesy of looking away while she put on a dressing gown.

She didn't challenge our presence. I believe she knew that she'd talked herself into trouble. When dressed, she did throw one very angry look in my direction and scream a series of very vulgar words not fit for a beautiful woman's mouth. It ended with a few unkind words for her handsome husband.

"Sorry we had to interfere with Peter's funeral, Adrianna. We'll make up for it by arranging yours."

* * *

Agosto shook Nan's hand and then mine. "Good work, you two. Tough one to crack, es verdad?"

"Very es verdad...whatever that means," Nan said.

"It sort of fell into our laps, Lieutenant. I don't know if we would have put it together without Sheri Parnell's suicide, Cromwell's trips to Virginia, and Victor's attempt to toast Nina Samuelson."

"Dustan's stupidity didn't help solve anything. Just a tangential piece of stupidity that sidetracked us some," Nan said.

"Tangential?" Agosto said. "Did you pick that up from the Rock?"

"Hardly," Nan responded. "The guy calls gams, legs. Do you believe it?"

"Gams?" Louis said. "What in the hell are gams?"

Epilogue

Seeking innocence on the streets of a city would be both a display of ingenuousness and an exercise in futility. If one truly seeks it, visit a nursery and look into the face of a sleeping   baby. Start and stop there and you'll never be disappointed.

CBW - 08

Epilogue

Four months have slid by since Adrianna and Peter Cromwell, Dan Shepherd, and Victor Parnell were sentenced: Victor received a death sentence; Peter and Dan Shepherd got twenty-five to life (Both testified against Adrianna); and Adrianna got life without the possibility of parole.

That out of the way, our baby was born a month ago and we named her after my mother, Janeen. Dad fights everyone to hold her. Takes her over to the office every day to show her off. Denise has eased her way into the family without friction. She and Midge have secrets. I guess that's a good sign. April and Midge speak, but can hardly be called friends. Or enemies.

Dad did buy his company back from Easterling. He still prepares bids with Mary Jane's help. However, he's turned the day-to-day oversight to the man he'd recommended to Easterling. Title: Manager of Operations. I've promised to take over when I get twenty five years in as a detective. He wants it to stay in the family. Has suggested that Midge and I get busy making a boy. We're amenable, but if the next is another beautiful little girl we'll keep her. And he'll love her and maybe groom her to be the president of Paxton Construction, Inc.

A final note, Hernando and Georgia have made it legal. Last week. We went to the wedding. Georgia was gorgeous and Hernando was still dancing with her when we departed at midnight. Luis was still around, pleased as punch and passing out illegal Cuban cigars in memory of his grandfather who he claims was a cattle rancher. Everyone at the shop knows that Gramps had rolled cigars for one of the several—now defunct—Ybor City Cigar manufacturers.

Every couple of months or so, I visit Dustan Samuelson, Sr. We've become friends. He's closed his college and travels a lot. I don't know why I care, but I do. He lost a son and a beautiful daughter. He and Dustan's wife, Nina, have bonded. That seems great for both of them. I've just begun to understand how much the loss of a child could hurt.

I'm finished now. Midge just glanced into the library and smiled. I believe I know what she wants. Que Sera Sera.

Rock Paxton

Printed in the United States
130921LV00001B/168/P